"...Alvin," said Speedy, "in the next five or six hours you can be the talk of the town *if you'll just take control.* If you'll just *be* Mayor Fernald."

"But how—" began Alvin.

"I'll tell you how. You have key kids in all the key offices in this town, just waiting for you to pick up the phone and tell them what to do. You have twenty-two other kids playing baseball and kickball over on the school grounds, eager to help you run this city. You have Shoie here, ready to carry any private messages for you on his bike, and he's the fastest bike rider in school—and you have my brains to work behind the scenes."

The Magnificent Brain began stirring into action. "You know," said Alvin thoughtfully, "we *might* be able to do something at that."

Alvin Fernald, Mayor for a Day
was originally published by
Holt, Rinehart and Winston.

About the Author and Illustrator:

CLIFFORD B. HICKS was born in Marshalltown, Iowa,
and graduated from Northwestern University. His
popular stories about Alvin are inspired by the antics
of his three sons, and include *The Marvelous Inven-
tions of Alvin Fernald; Alvin's Secret Code;* and *Alvin
Fernald, Foreign Trader.* Mr. Hicks is also an editor
of a scientific and mechanical magazine and lives with
his family in Elmhurst, Illinois.

BILL SOKOL is an Associate Art Director of *The New
York Times* and has always been keenly interested in
graphics. His work has been cited by the Art Directors
Club and the American Institute of Graphic Arts.

Alvin Fernald, Mayor for a Day

by Clifford B. Hicks

Illustrated by Bill Sokol

AN ARCHWAY PAPERBACK
POCKET BOOKS • NEW YORK

ALVIN FERNALD, MAYOR FOR A DAY

Archway Paperback edition published August, 1971

L

Published by
POCKET BOOKS, a division of Simon & Schuster, Inc.,
630 Fifth Avenue, New York, N.Y.

Archway Paperback editions are distributed in the U.S.
by Simon & Schuster, Inc., 630 Fifth Avenue, New
York, N.Y. 10020 and in Canada by Simon & Schuster
of Canada, Ltd., Richmond Hill, Ontario, Canada.

Standard Book Number: 671-29509-8.
Library of Congress Catalog Card Number: 70-80325.

FOR AL AND LOUISE —

who have helped much more than they realize

Contents

1. If I Were Mayor—   1
2. Speedy Glomitz, Master Politician   6
3. Campaign Strategy   12
4. The Candidate Gives His Speech   18
5. A Triumphant Ride   29
6. Alvin Takes Office   36
7. What About Those Campaign Promises?   42
8. The Mayor Goes into Action   47
9. A Mysterious Leatherbound Book   56
10. A Difference in Dimensions   68
11. A Message to the FBI   76
12. Discovered!   85
13. Locked In!   89
14. Whummmmp!   95
15. Emergency Plan   100
16. Preparations for an Ambush   111
17. Conversation on a Tree Limb   117
18. Captured!   121
19. A Shortage in the City Treasury   136

Alvin Fernald, Mayor for a Day

1

If I Were Mayor—

Mayor Alvin Fernald. . . .

It had a nice ring to it, thought Alvin, like "President George Washington" or "General Robert E. Lee." He might *really* run for Mayor of Riverton some day. It would be a wad of fun to ride around in the Mayor's long black car, with a motorcycle out in front. He'd be tall and very distinguished, with gray hair, and he'd wave at everyone as he passed.

Mayor Alvin Fernald. . . .

"Alvin!"

Miss Pinkney's voice broke into his thoughts. Mentally, he leaped out of the long black car and back to his desk in the Fifth Grade, Room 3B, Roosevelt School. And the tall, distinguished-looking man became Alvin Fernald, slim and short for an eleven-year-old, freckles splattering his face, his short brown hair bristling in every direction like a worn-out toothbrush.

"Alvin, do you suppose you could rejoin the class long enough to answer my question?"

A couple of the girls giggled. Everyone in class was aware of Alvin's daydreams.

"What question, Miss Pinkney?"

"I asked you whether you knew what form of city government we have here in Riverton."

"Well. . . . Uh. . . . Well, we have a Mayor and we have, let's see, we have the police and fire departments, and, uh, then there's the men who pick up the garbage."

There was another giggle from the back row of desks.

"Alvin, you were the one who suggested that we have political parties here in class, and elect our own Mayor. It's a fine idea. But I expect you to pay attention, so you'll learn *why* we have political parties, what city officials we have in Riverton, and what their duties are. Now, Theresa, what form of government do we have in our city?"

Theresa always knows the answers, thought Alvin. Somehow it irritated him.

"In Riverton we have a mayor-council form of government. Riverton is divided into areas, called wards. The voters in each ward elect a person to represent them on the city council. And all the voters in town elect a Mayor—the head of the city government."

A Mayor, the head of the city government. Mayor Alvin Fernald. . . . Actually, he *should* be Mayor—

at least in class—because it had been his idea in the first place.

He'd made the suggestion a few minutes ago, when Miss Pinkney had told them to put away their math books because it was time for social studies. "For the next three weeks," she'd said, "we'll be studying our local government. At the end of that time—you'd better make a note of this, class—I'll expect each of you to hand in a five-page report telling how Riverton is governed."

"Geeeeeeez!" The exclamation came from Shoie's throat in a hoarse whisper. Shoie was Alvin's best friend. He was known as the Mighty Athlete of Roosevelt School. He could run faster, throw a ball farther and stand on his head until his face got purpler than anyone else in school.

But Shoie could not write themes.

"That will be enough, Wilfred." Shoie's real name was Wilfred Shoemaker. "You will all write a theme on Riverton's city government."

"Miss Pinkney!" Alvin didn't know what he was going to say, but as usual he felt he should help out his best friend.

"Yes, Alvin?"

"Couldn't we—well—I mean—couldn't we just sort of talk about what we would do if we were Mayor of Riverton, instead of writing it all down?"

"You mean, could you give a campaign speech for the office of Mayor?"

"Yeah. I mean, yes—I guess that's what I mean."

There was a moment of silence while Miss Pinkney thought this over. Finally she said, "What about that, class? Would the rest of you rather give campaign speeches, or write themes?"

Everyone voted for speeches except Worm Wormley, who stuttered. Alvin looked at him thoughtfully. Suddenly he had another inspiration.

"Miss Pinkney, couldn't just a few of us give speeches, and the others help?"

"I think what you're asking, Alvin, is whether you could form political parties."

"Yeah, that's what I mean. And couldn't we see who *really* gets elected Mayor—at least right here in class?"

There was another pause. Alvin saw Miss Pinkney glance at Worm Wormley for just a split second, then look at Alvin. He thought he saw a faint smile of understanding on her face. "I think that's a fine suggestion, Alvin. But it's going to take a lot of study.

"First, you'll have to find out about the Riverton city government, so you'll know how it's governed, and what its problems are. Then you'll divide yourself into groups—political parties—depending upon how you would solve those problems. Finally, you'll nominate your candidates. Each candidate will give a campaign speech telling what he'd do if he were Mayor. After that, we'll have the election."

"If I were Mayor, I'd—" began Alvin.

"You don't know anything about being Mayor yet, Alvin. I suggest you do some studying. Starting

4

tomorrow, I'll set aside a half hour each day. As soon as you've formed your political parties, you can start working on your platforms. Does anyone know what a platform is?"

"I'll b-b-b-b-bring the hammer and nails," offered Worm.

"Not that kind of a platform," said Miss Pinkney patiently. "A political platform is a written statement. It tells what the party thinks, as a group, about the government. It also tells what the party will do if its candidate is elected." She paused, looking around the room. "There'll be plenty of work for everyone. Some of you will be working on party platforms, some will be working behind the scenes for your candidates."

As she spoke those words, Alvin happened to be looking at Speedy Glomitz. Speedy's eyes were moving slowly up one row of students and down another. Those eyes were half-closed most of the time, like the eyes of a turtle. When Speedy's eyes came to Alvin, they stopped. Alvin found himself staring straight into the turtle-eyes. Then he noticed that the tip of Speedy's tongue had slipped slowly out of the corner of his mouth. Speedy chewed on it for a moment, as though trying to decide something. Alvin watched, almost hypnotized, as the tongue disappeared, and the corners of Speedy's mouth turned up in a slow grin.

The incident made Alvin nervous. In fact, everything about Speedy Glomitz made Alvin nervous.

2

Speedy Glomitz, Master Politician

Speedy was almost the only kid Alvin had ever met that he couldn't understand.

Some kids, Alvin sensed, want everything for themselves. Some want to be big-shots (Alvin had to admit that *he* had a tendency in this direction). Some have to win at everything they do. Some are loners. Some want to be in the middle of a gang. There are a good many kinds of kids, thought Alvin, and if you know what kind of a kid a kid is, you pretty much know what he'll do, and why.

But not Speedy. Speedy was a complete mystery. It wasn't that Alvin disliked him. In fact, Speedy was rather fascinating—but it was like being fascinated by a snapping turtle. You never knew when he was going to snap.

And Alvin had been bitten several times. At least he had been outwitted by Speedy, and that, according to Shoie, took someone who was super-smart. Shoie frequently referred to Alvin's mind as the

Magnificent Brain, because it seemed to flash with wild and unpredictable ideas, like a computer out of control.

Speedy, though, often managed to outwit the Magnificent Brain.

There was the time when six of the guys who lived along Elm Street had decided to form a club. Alvin took it for granted that he would be elected president. After all, hadn't the club been his idea? And weren't the guys sitting on his front lawn while they were planning it? And anyway, wouldn't he make the *best* president?

But just as they were getting ready to vote, Speedy asked two questions in that slow, lazy voice of his:

"Worm, how's business at your old man's ice cream shop?"

And, "Anybody want to play football this afternoon?"

Well, you'd think the other kids would see through those questions. But they didn't. They all figured that if Worm was president of the club, all of the members would get free ice cream sodas. And they all knew that Worm owned the only football, except for Shoie's tired one with the bulge on one side.

So Speedy, with just two questions, managed to get Worm elected president, and then he and Worm, instead of playing football, walked off downtown, where they each guzzled two free ice cream sodas.

Another time, in fourth grade, Speedy had outfoxed Alvin. Miss Davis had suggested that the class do something special, outside their regular school-work, and asked for ideas.

Speedy suggested they raise tropical fish. (Alvin knew why Speedy had made the suggestion; he had a big aquarium at home, and the whole class would look to him for leadership in the project.)

Alvin suggested that they start a school news-paper. After a great deal of argument between the boys, Alvin was surprised when Speedy suddenly gave in. Speedy said he thought the newspaper was a fine idea—and that Theresa Undermine would make a good editor.

Alvin was amazed. After all, the newspaper had been *his* idea, so *he* should be editor. Besides, Theresa was so shy she only spoke in a faint whisper. Most of the time, it was as though Theresa wasn't even *there*.

But that year the girls had outnumbered the boys, and all the girls voted for Theresa. Alvin had to admit that Theresa had done a good job as editor. Furthermore, the job had helped her break out of her shell of shyness. In fact, Theresa had broken so *far* out of her shell that now you couldn't shut her up.

She'd done a good job, Alvin recalled, except for that long article she'd run in the newspaper about Speedy and his tropical fish. She'd made it sound like such an exciting hobby that, sure enough, all the kids came flocking around Speedy to learn how to set up their own aquariums. And Alvin had felt completely left out—no job as editor, and everyone looking to Speedy as the big shot of the class.

No, Alvin couldn't understand Speedy Glomitz as he sat there in the classroom. Speedy never seemed to want anything for himself. But he always seemed to *get* things for himself, by sort of pushing and pulling other people behind the scenes.

Alvin was sure of one thing. *Speedy wasn't going to keep him from being elected Mayor of Riverton.*

That's why he was so surprised at what happened on the way home from school. He and Shoie were walking along Elm Street, talking about the forthcoming election, when they heard a whistle like a bluejay behind them. Without looking, they both knew it was Speedy. He was the only guy who could whistle like that, because of the triangular gap between his two front teeth.

They waited for him. He ambled slowly along the sidewalk, a rather short and stocky boy, his head swinging from side to side on his long neck, like a turtle looking back and forth. In fact, all of his movements were just about as slow as a turtle's. That's why the kids called him Speedy.

"You're it, Alvin," Speedy said, as he approached.

"I'm what?" Alvin asked suspiciously.

"You're it. You're the Mayor. Ooooorrrrf." Speedy was always making very strange sounds in the back of his mouth, eerie sounds that seemed to come from nowhere. Yet they sort of punctuated his words, giving additional meaning to them.

9

"How do you *know* I'll be Mayor? We didn't even hear about the election until today."

"I'll fix it. You'll be the Mayor." There wasn't a shade of doubt in Speedy's voice.

Alvin found himself saying, "Mayor Fernald." Then he said it again, more slowly this time. "Mayor Fernald. It would be kind of nice." Suddenly an alarm bell went off inside his Magnificent Brain. He said suspiciously, "Suppose you could fix it somehow. Why would you help me, instead of trying to be Mayor yourself? And what do you expect to get out of it?"

The lazy eyes blinked at Alvin. "I don't want to be Mayor, Alvin. All I want is the fun of making someone else Mayor. And I can fix it. You'll see."

3

Campaign Strategy

During the next couple of weeks there were some excited meetings in the classroom. Occasionally the arguments got so loud that Mr. Wachholz, the principal, had to walk into the room, clear his throat, teeter up on his toes, and then walk out again.

Almost by accident, the class divided itself into two even groups. Speedy managed to get one group to meet each day around Alvin's desk, so Alvin found himself the center of attention. The other group met off in one corner of the room, where Theresa Undermine's voice was louder than all the others.

Speedy suggested to Alvin, one morning before school, that they should name their group the Young Citizens' Party. Alvin didn't think the name was so hot, but when Speedy asked him later, during the meeting around his desk, what they should name the party, Alvin couldn't think of anything better, so he said, "The Young Citizens' Party." Then he acted proud of the suggestion.

After all these discussions around his desk, it was only natural that, on the day of nominations, Alvin Fernald found himself candidate for Mayor on the Young Citizens' Party ticket. It was a unanimous decision, thanks to Speedy's work behind the scenes.

Alvin's opponent in the election turned out to be Theresa Undermine. She had named her party The-People's-Party-for-Making-Riverton-a-More-Desirable-and-Prosperous-City-in-Which-to-Live. It sounded just like Theresa, thought Alvin. Ever since she'd been editor of the school paper, she used a whole batch of words when one would have been enough.

Two days before the election, while the kids were still working on their party platforms, Miss Pinkney made a surprise announcement.

"Children, we have a problem. The election apparently will end in a tie, because fifteen of you are working for Theresa and fifteen for Alvin. There's no real purpose in campaigning because all of you now are working for one of the candidates. You simply don't have any voters left in this room to convince.

"After thinking about this problem for several days, I called Mayor Massey's office at City Hall. I discussed the problem with Mayor Massey himself. His response was immediate. He has agreed to come here, a week from today, and listen to the campaign speeches by the candidates for Mayor. He then will decide the winner himself."

During the momentary silence that followed, Alvin thought to himself, *I wonder what I'll say in my speech.*

Miss Pinkney broke into his thoughts:

"I have an even more exciting announcement to make. The Mayor is so pleased with our project that he has decided the winner really *will* become Mayor of Riverton for one day. He will sit in the Mayor's office. He will appoint members of this class as the other public officials."

Cheers from all the kids!

Mayor for a day, thought Alvin. *I'm going to be Mayor of Riverton for one whole day.*

It didn't turn out to be that easy.

Two days later, Bigmouth Snodgrass, who belonged to the other party and couldn't keep his mouth shut, bragged that Theresa was sure to win because she'd already written her speech and it was a real shouter.

After school, Speedy made a suggestion. "Alvin, why don't you have Shoie walk past Theresa's house tonight?"

"Why?"

"Well, Shoie might happen to hear her practicing her speech. Then we'll know what we're up against."

That night, Alvin and Speedy were waiting under the streetlight when Shoie came back with his report. His eyes were dazed, as though he'd just been handed a report card covered with A's. Alvin had to bonk him on the head or he would have walked right past, without even seeing the other two boys.

"Well, did you hear her speech?" asked Alvin.

"Wow, can that girl talk up a storm," Shoie said softly. "It made me want to stand right up and shout."

"What was she talking about?" asked Speedy in his slow drawl.

"Oh, all about our country, and the flag, and —and—well, I don't really remember what she said, but the *way* she said it sure gave me the shivers."

"That's our answer," said Speedy. "Alvin, you've got to be right down to earth in your speech. You've got to give facts, facts and more facts, so Mayor Massey can tell that you know all about Riverton and how to run it. You've got to promise four or five very specific things you'll do as Mayor, things that *need* doing, and nobody can argue with. That's your only chance. You've got to promise *action*. Matter of fact, that's a pretty good slogan to work into your speech. 'A vote for Alvin is a vote for ACTION!' "

" 'A vote for Alvin is a vote for ACTION!' " repeated Alvin. "Hey, that's great!" Then a black cloud settled down over the Magnificent Brain. "But I don't *know* lots of facts about Riverton. And I don't *know* what should be done for the town."

Speedy said quietly, "I've had some of the other kids digging up facts for days, while you've been trying to get votes for the nomination. And I know

15

exactly how you can win Mayor Massey's vote, and therefore win the election."

"How?"

"Well, Mayor Massey himself has to run for reelection in about three months. He's out for all the publicity he can get, starting right now. Otherwise, why would he agree to visit our classroom? I'll bet he'll have a photographer along, and there'll be lots of pictures in the paper that night showing the Mayor with us kids."

"Great!" said Alvin. The Magnificent Brain was already posing for pictures. "But I don't see how that will help *me* win *my* election."

"The Mayor already has a program for *his* election. You just take that over—at least part of it— in your speech. The Mayor is promising more stop signs for safety; you promise that, too. The Mayor is promising more and bigger playgrounds for the kids of Riverton; you promise that, too. Then, by choosing you as Mayor for a Day, he'll get lots of publicity for his *own* program. See how it works?"

"Maybe," Alvin said grudgingly. He was awed by the way Speedy's mind could run in circles and loops, like a snake, and come up with the right answer. But at the same time, Speedy bothered him. Speedy had taken over his entire campaign. Still, he couldn't resist asking, "What about my campaign speech?"

"Don't worry. I'll write that for you. All you have to do is practice delivering it. I'll write a speech that will make you Mayor of Riverton."

"Yowwweee!" shouted Shoie, turning a handspring on the grass beneath the streetlight. "Alvin's going to be Mayor!"

"There's only one thing I want in return, Alvin," said Speedy. "When you're Mayor for a Day, I don't want any office, or anything like that, but I *do* want to be able to walk in and out of *your* office anytime I want. Okay?"

Alvin was suspicious, but didn't see how Speedy could cause him any trouble with this simple request. "Okay," he promised.

It was a promise he was to regret more than once.

4

The Candidate Gives His Speech

Alvin was seated at his desk, the applause ringing in his ears. The trouble was, it was applause for Theresa, not for him.

Oh, she'd given a good speech all right—a real shouter. She'd ended up reciting some of the words from "The Star-Spangled Banner," words that even brought shivers to Alvin's spine. There'd been a long moment of silence, and now everybody was clapping like mad.

The Mayor, who had been seated in a chair at one side of the room, stood up. He walked toward Theresa, a smile on his handsome face, gold-rimmed glasses gleaming, his graying hair carefully parted. Alvin noticed that most of the kids were watching him instead of Theresa. Or they were watching the photographer, who was working his way around the classroom snapping pictures.

The Mayor took Theresa's hand, but as he did so he thrust himself just a bit in front of her, so he would be the center of attention in the photos. It made Alvin mad. After all, whose election was this?

As a matter of fact, there was something about Mayor Massey that disturbed Alvin a bit, though he couldn't figure out exactly what it was. The Mayor was just a little too slick, too much of an operator. Alvin found himself distrusting the man for no real reason.

The applause for Theresa was so long and so loud that Alvin had the sinking feeling he'd already lost.

Now it was his turn. He wriggled out of his desk and walked to the front of the room. He tried to reassure himself that he'd do a good job. All he had to do was give the speech as Speedy had taught it to him.

When he turned around, though, and saw all those faces looking at him, he suddenly froze. His Magnificent Brain clicked off as though someone had pulled the electric plug. About the only thought that seemed to come through was the realization that his knees were beginning to shake.

The longer he stood there, the quieter the room became. He opened his mouth once in an effort to speak, but there seemed to be a fuzzy cold ball blocking his throat, so he closed his mouth again.

Some girl in the back of the room started to giggle, breaking the silence, and suddenly everyone was laughing.

Strangely, it was Worm Wormley who rescued him, Worm the stutterer. Worm had heard Alvin practice his speech. Now, sitting in the front row, he leaned forward and said in a loud whisper, "T-t-t-t-tell them about the p-p-p-p-playgrounds, Alvin!"

The laughter in the room had suddenly stopped, and although Worm made his suggestion in a whisper, the stuttering sentence came out like a shout. Immediately everyone started roaring again, this time at Worm as well as Alvin. Bigmouth Snodgrass was laughing so hard the tears were rolling down his face.

But, thanks to Worm, the Magnificent Brain had clicked into action. Suddenly, Alvin was thinking clearly. Let them laugh, he thought. He'd make a speech they'd remember for a long time.

As the laughter finally died down, he began. "My good friends and fellow citizens of Riverton," he said, his voice shaking just a bit. "A vote for Alvin is a vote for ACTION!" He cleared his throat, then quickly went on. "Yes, ACTION is what I promise you, ACTION to improve this town in which we live."

It encouraged him that the classroom finally had fallen silent. He noticed that Miss Pinkney, who was seated by the Mayor, had a look of pride on her face as she watched.

"I want to tell you what I would do if I were Mayor for a Day. First, we don't have enough playgrounds for the kids." He slipped smoothly into the speech Speedy had written. "Members of the Citizens' Party have found out that Riverton has fewer playgrounds than any city of its size in the state. Yet we have many vacant lots covered with weeds. When I'm Mayor, we'll get the kids to mow and rake those lots, and we'll put baseball diamonds on them."

A loud cheer went up from Shoie, the Mighty Athlete. All the boys in the room started clapping.

"And let's not forget the girls," Alvin went on when the applause died down. "Last year a little girl, while riding her bicycle down the street, was killed. The Citizens' Party found out that it was called an 'unavoidable accident.' But it *was* avoidable. All we needed was a stop sign at Maple and Third Streets. Why isn't there a stop sign there? Well, the trucks from the quarry, out on the edge of town, use Third Street all the time. When a stop sign was suggested, the quarry convinced the City Council that it wasn't really needed. That's what the Citizens' Party found out, by talking to our councilmen. The first thing we'll do, when I'm Mayor, is put up a stop sign there—and maybe some other places, too. Then the kids of Riverton can ride their bikes safely. It's time somebody paid attention to us kids!"

A roar of approval went up from the class.

Alvin went smoothly ahead with his speech. He'd memorized it so well that, now that he'd started, he found his mind drifting. Once, while looking at the Mayor, he wondered why some of these things hadn't already been done. They shouldn't be very difficult.

He ticked off other things he'd do as Mayor, things Speedy had written into his speech. He'd add new routes for the city buses. There was a city law against peddlers going from house to house, and he'd make sure it was obeyed. He pointed out that Mrs. Mulrooney had recently been talking to one peddler at the front door while another had slipped through the back door and stolen her money.

"I promise I'll do all these things when I am the Mayor," Alvin said, approaching the end of his speech.

Then he let his voice sink almost to a whisper, as Speedy had told him to do, and spoke very slowly, "And these aren't just promises. As soon as I step into the Mayor's office, I'll start working on them. A vote for me is a vote for ACTION! Thank you."

The classroom rang with applause. The Mayor stood up, clapping, a broad smile on his handsome face, and walked across to Alvin. His big hand fell around Alvin's shoulder, as though he himself were taking credit for Alvin's performance.

Mayor Massey held up his hand for silence. When the class had quieted down, he said, "Young man, that was one of the finest speeches I've ever heard. You promised the citizens of this beautiful town exactly what I hope to do in my next term of office. And the good citizens of Riverton deserve the very best."

Gosh, thought Alvin, *he's going into a campaign speech of his own.* He could hear the scratch of the pencil as Mr. Bronski, the newspaper reporter, took down every word. Speedy had been right. Mayor

Massey was using the class as a means of getting himself reelected. Somehow, it didn't seem quite fair.

"And I want you to know, Alvin, that I too am a man of action. Right now I'm working to accomplish many of the things you have recommended, but you children must understand that some of these things take time. You must be patient, and we'll work them out. Within six months, I'm sure, we can get some of them done."

Again Alvin heard the scratch of the reporter's pencil. In six months, if Mayor Massey were re-elected, he would be well into his second term. Alvin couldn't see why it should take more than a few days to put up some stop signs, mow some vacant lots, reroute a few buses and enforce a law against ped-dlers. He was about to say something, then decided against it.

"Now it is my honor—and duty—to select a win-ner. This is very difficult to do. Miss Undermine, will you please come forward?"

Lights flashed on and off in the Magnificent Brain, as though it had been short-circuited.

Theresa stood on one side of Mayor Massey and Alvin on the other. The tall man put his arms around both of them.

"Miss Undermine, you gave one of the most rous-ing speeches I've ever heard. Congratulations. I hope you'll join me on the platform, on the Fourth of July, and give a five-minute speech to the citizens."

Theresa can't possibly limit herself to five minutes of speech-making, thought Alvin. Then his mind came back to the present. The Mayor *still* hadn't announced the winner.

"Mr. Alvin Fernald, because you came up with concrete recommendations to improve this beautiful city, and because you promise, as a man of action, to carry through those recommendations, I hereby declare you the winner, and Mayor for a Day, of Riverton, Indiana!"

All the members of the Young Citizens' Party whooped it up. Shoie pounded Spider Funsterman on the back, almost doubling him over. Worm Wormley shouted "G-g-g-g-g-great!" Speedy sat in the back row, a sly smile on his face.

"Now, Alvin," said the Mayor, "I don't suppose you'd object to a few flashbulbs going off at this time, would you?" Everyone laughed, and the Mayor beckoned the photographer forward.

Alvin could feel that arm around his shoulder pushing him to one side, just a bit, so the Mayor would be in the center of the picture. He pushed back, and just before the flashbulb went off he leaned his head to one side so it would be right in front of the camera. Alvin didn't like being pushed around, even by the Mayor.

After several pictures had been taken—some with Theresa, some with Miss Pinkney, some with all the members of the Young Citizens' Party—the Mayor once again held up his hand for silence.

"I regret that I must leave now." He coughed self-consciously. "Must get about our city's business, you know. However, before I leave I want to arrange

with Alvin to take over the city administration, at least for one day. I don't believe you can get in much trouble in one day, Alvin." Everyone laughed except Alvin.

"As a matter of fact, I've already picked the day, Saturday, April 28. Because it's a Saturday, there won't be much business that requires your attention. And besides," he added with a smile, "that's the date of the annual City Officials' Golf Tournament, so we won't be around to get in your way."

As the Mayor spoke these words, Alvin happened to be looking at Speedy. A slow, easy smile spread across Speedy's face, as though he already had some plans that no one knew about.

"Alvin, between now and April 28 you may appoint all your other city officials from the children in this room. And the entire class is invited to my office at nine o'clock that morning. We'll have a *Daily Bugle* photographer there. I'll have each of my city officials meet his corresponding student official, and fill him in on his duties. Then you kids can govern the city for the day, while the rest of us go play golf."

Mayor Massey strode to the door, waving to the kids. Just before he departed, he looked back and winked broadly at Alvin. "Don't forget. Promptly at nine o'clock, Mayor Fernald!"

Mayor Fernald, thought Alvin, as he walked out the school door. It certainly had a nice ring. . . .

As he headed across the schoolyard, Alicia Malienchowicsky came running up behind him. "Alvin," she said excitedly, "Alvin, when are you going to get my name in the paper, guaranteed spelled right, like you promised?"

Spider Funsterman was right behind her. "Alvin, I hope you remember that I get to be starting pitcher against Edison School. I don't know how you're going to arrange that with Mr. Feeney, but you promised!"

Alvin didn't know what to say. "What do you mean, I promised you those things? I don't know what you're talking about."

"Well," said Alicia, "maybe *you* didn't promise them, but Speedy did. He promised that if I'd help you become Mayor, you'd get my name in the paper. He promised Spider he could pitch in the game against Edison. And he promised Worm a new wheel for his bicycle, the wheel that's hanging in your garage."

Alvin was stunned. Now he knew why some of the kids had worked so hard for the Young Citizens' Party. Just then Speedy came ambling up to the group.

"Speedy, what are we going to do?" asked Alvin. "I mean, you promised—" He waved his hand toward Alicia and Spider.

Speedy smiled slowly, his eyelids drooping. "Well, Alvin, this is what is known in politics as the spoils system. My dad told me about it. Those that work for you get something out of it. Now, let's see what kind of a deal we can work out."

Alvin stood, pop-eyed, while Speedy succeeded in talking himself out of his promises. He did it by appointing Spider the Commissioner of Public Works in Alvin's administration, and Alicia the City Treasurer. Alvin could only nod when Speedy asked him if the appointments were okay. As a matter of fact, Alvin thought, Alicia probably would make a good treasurer; she understood the sets and functions of modern math better than anyone else in class.

Mayor Fernald. The nice ring of it struck him again as he and Speedy walked away. He looked out the corner of his eye at the other boy and said it aloud. "Mayor Fernald. Yep, Speedy, I guess we did a pretty good job in that old political campaign. And I sure do want to thank you for your help."

There was a long silence. Then Speedy said, "There'll be plenty of time for that later. Meanwhile we have lots of work to do. Yeah, we have lots of work ahead of us."

The remark puzzled Alvin, and even more, it angered him. Particularly the "we" part. After all, *he* was going to be the Mayor. *He* was going to run the city—for one whole day. Speeches, interviews, photos.

It was going to be a lot of fun.

5

A Triumphant Ride

"My good friends and fellow citizens of Riverton—"

Today was the day.

Alvin hadn't been able to eat much for breakfast because he was so excited. Now he was practicing his "speech of acceptance," which he hoped to give in the Mayor's office.

His face looked back at him from the cracked mirror on his bedroom wall. It wasn't a particularly dignified face. In fact, it was just the opposite. It was covered with uneven clusters of freckles, as though he'd been spattered by the Hickory Street guys in a mudfight. And there were more freckles on one side than the other, giving his face a strange, lopsided look. Shoie had once said that Alvin's face only looked right if you tilted your head while viewing it.

No, it didn't look like a Mayor's face. Still, on this fine Saturday morning late in April, he really *was* the Mayor, and he was preparing to go to his office at the City Hall in Riverton, Indiana.

Mayor of 35,381 citizens (according to the highway sign on the edge of town).

Mayor Alvin Fernald.

Alvin finished knotting his necktie. It was the only one he owned—he'd picked it out himself—and it was covered with modernistic orange owls that seemed to leap out of a bright blue background. It matched his face, he thought, in a moment of honesty. Not very dignified.

Finally he stepped back from the mirror for an over-all look. The results weren't very reassuring. Either the sleeves of his sport coat were too short, or his arms were too long. He tried to correct this condition by pulling his arms up inside his sleeves, but this pushed his shoulders up around his ears so he looked like he didn't have any neck.

While trying to stretch the jacket sleeves, he could hear the Pest (his name for his little sister Daphne) humming to herself in the room next door as she prepared to go with him to City Hall.

Suddenly he heard the wail of a police siren. He dashed to the window and looked down just as the patrol car came to a halt in front of the house, the siren dying to a low moan. A sign had been installed atop the patrol car. In big red letters it said, "Mayor Massey Welcomes Alvin Fernald as Mayor for a Day."

The sight made Alvin's pulse jump with excitement, but he couldn't help noticing that Mayor Massey's name appeared first on the sign.

Now he watched as his father, Sergeant John

Fernald of the Riverton Police Department, got out of the patrol car. Dad had requested—and been granted—the honor of driving Alvin to the City Hall. He was a wiry little man, and he waved cheerfully up at Alvin standing in the bedroom window.

"Come on down, Mr. Mayor," he shouted. "Time to put in a good day's work."

It was obvious that Sergeant Fernald was very proud of Alvin, at least most of the time, despite all the scrapes and troubles that resulted from the ideas that came tumbling out of the Magnificent Brain. Usually it was Dad who helped rescue him from these disasters.

"He's here, Daddy's here!" shouted the Pest through the door. "Come on, Alvin, it's time to leave!"

"Plenty of time," he called. "We're not due until nine o'clock."

"Nine o'clock," she repeated. His little sister had the habit of repeating the last thing she heard, like some small mysterious echo. Now, as he opened the door, she was standing there in a bright yellow dress, her hair combed into long blond curls that hung around her shoulders, a yellow ribbon perched on her head.

It was a pleasant surprise to see her so neatly dressed. Usually, except when she was in school, she wore a pair of shorts she had made by cutting off the legs of his outgrown jeans, and an old sweatshirt that Beanball Bagley, the hero of the high school baseball team, had given her when she boldly

31

knocked on his door and asked for it. The Pest was a tomboy, which worried her mother a great deal.

This morning Alvin was proud of her as she stood there, neat as a pin, waiting for him. Momentarily he was glad he had named her "Personal Secretary to the Mayor," even though she was only in third grade.

She had begged him to give her the job so she could, as she put it, "be where the action is."

"Let's go," he said.

"Let's go!" she repeated. "Let's go, Your Highness." She wasn't quite sure how to address a Mayor.

Dad saluted, a proud smile on his face, when Alvin approached the squad car. With a sweep of his arm he opened the rear door, and made sure Alvin and Daphne were comfortable before closing it behind them. He even turned on the blinking dome light, and promised to turn on the siren while they drove through the business district. It was a real thrill for Alvin because his father never let him ride in the squad car.

As they turned the corner at Oak Street, Alvin said, "Dad, what do you think of Mayor Massey?"

"Why do you ask?"

"I dunno. I was just thinking about him. Do you know him very well?"

"Pretty well. He drops into Police Headquarters frequently. Seems to like to spend time there when he's not busy. What do *you* think of him, Alvin?"

"Seems like everything he does is to help *him*, and not somebody else."

"Well, Alvin, he's up for reelection soon. So maybe he's just campaigning." There was a pause. Then, "But I know what you mean. Just between us—and don't ever repeat it—I'm not very enthusiastic about Mayor Massey either. But a lot of the local businessmen are."

"Has he lived in Riverton all his life?"

"Matter of fact, he hasn't lived here very long—only about six years. But within two years after his arrival, he'd shaken so many hands, joined so many organizations, and talked so much about his past experience in government that someone suggested he run for Mayor. He ran, and won. As soon as he took over the Mayor's office, he sent for his former secretary, Miss Carner. Together, they've sort of run Riverton ever since."

"Has he been a good Mayor, Dad?"

"Depends on how you look at it. He's put through some big improvements—the new swimming pool, and now the new City Hall that's under construction." Another pause. "But it doesn't seem to me that the average citizen, if he has a complaint, ever gets heard. Mayor Massey insists that all complaints come directly to his office. Miss Carner handles them, and always promises to do something about the problem. But nothing ever seems to get done."

"I don't particularly like the Mayor," said Alvin.

"Don't like the Mayor," said the Pest.

"Well, keep your thoughts to yourselves, kids. And don't repeat what I've told you. Mayor Massey is probably a good enough man—just self-centered."

As Dad swung the car onto Main Street, he turned on the siren. Still, he kept the speed slow, just crawling along, as they entered the business district. Early shoppers and businessmen looked up, grinned at the sign, and started waving and cheering. Alvin sat up on the edge of the seat, where he could be seen better, rolled down the window, and waved back. He even cheered a little himself.

"Now who's self-centered?" asked Dad with a smile.

They drove through the business district, past the foundation for the new City Hall. Looking ahead, Alvin could see Miss Pinkney and all the kids of Room 3B waiting for him on the broad step of the old city building. A tremendous cheer went up as the squad car pulled up to the curb.

Alvin opened the door. Then he remembered, and quickly slammed it shut again. Dad came around the squad car and reopened it with a magnificent sweep of his arm.

Alvin and the Pest got out. Another cheer, even louder this time.

"Hi, gang!" Alvin said. They seemed to expect something more, and he didn't know what to say. "Well——. Well, here we are. Here's our big chance. The kids of Riverton are taking over." Then something inside forced him to be honest. "And I guess I'm kind of scared. I'm going to need lots of help."

Cheers and shouts.

He stood up straight. "Well, anyway, let's go find the Mayor's office!"

Another cheer, followed by much jostling up the steps.

Dad made sure that Miss Pinkney and Alvin went through the revolving door first. They walked down the long, broad corridor, past Police Headquarters, up the stairs to the second floor, and into the Mayor's reception room.

The first thing that Alvin saw was Speedy Glomitz sitting in the biggest leather chair in the room, his head scrunched over to one side and one leg thrown over the arm of the chair.

He looked like he owned the place.

6

Alvin Takes Office

Speedy was talking to the reporter and photographer from the *Daily Bugle*. Instantly Alvin was furious. How come Speedy had to be the first to appear in the Mayor's office? After all, *he* wasn't the Mayor today!

Speedy looked up and waved his arm lazily. "Hi, Alvin. I've been telling these men something about you—your childhood, where you went to school, and all that. I guess maybe you need a press agent."

Alvin opened his mouth to speak when a voice from the far corner of the room said, "Good morning, children. Good morning, Mayor Fernald."

Alvin saw a tall, handsome woman, her hair just beginning to turn gray, walk out from behind her desk. She crossed the room toward them. "And good morning to you, Miss Pinkney. I trust your class is ready to take over the city for a day?" She had a pretty face, but Alvin noticed there were faint lines around her mouth, as though she seldom smiled.

"I hope so," replied Miss Pinkney. "Alvin, I'd like you to meet Miss Carner, the Mayor's personal secretary."

"How do you do," said Alvin, just as someone accidentally shoved him from behind. He flew two feet forward and ended up in Miss Carner's arms.

Flustered, he said, "I'm sorry. Doggone it, Shoie, quit shoving."

"Worm shoved me!" retorted Shoie. "I couldn't help it."

"That's all right," said Miss Carner, carefully straightening her dress. She forced a smile. "I suppose kids are full of enthusiasm. If you'll wait, I'll see if Mayor Massey is ready to receive you." She disappeared through a paneled door.

He'd better be ready, thought Alvin. *After all, he's not the Mayor today—I am.*

Miss Carner promptly returned and said, "The Mayor will see you now, children."

The Mayor's office was at least twice the size of Alvin's living room. Part of one wall was covered with beautifully finished walnut filing cabinets. Underfoot, the carpet felt six inches thick.

In one corner, seated around a coffee table, were six men.

"Greetings, Mayor Fernald," said Mayor Massey, rising from behind his desk with a smile. "Come in, come in. Good morning, Miss Pinkney. I want your whole class here when Alvin takes office."

The rest of the kids pushed into the room behind Alvin.

"Now, Alvin," said Mayor Massey, "if you'll stand behind the desk here with me, we'll have some pictures taken so the good citizens of the city will know what their Mayor—at least for a day—looks like."

Alvin again posed with the Mayor as the flash-bulbs popped.

After the *Daily Bugle* photographer had taken a dozen shots, Mayor Massey motioned him away. "And now I'd like you children to meet my 'cabinet' —the other officials of your city. And Alvin, you can introduce your own officials who will take over their duties for today."

As the Mayor introduced each man, he stood up. Alvin then named the kid who would take his place. Spider Funsterman would be the Commissioner of Public Works, of course, and Alicia Maliencho-wicsky the City Treasurer (as Speedy had promised); Hortense Pillsberry would be the City Clerk because she had worked hard during Alvin's campaign; Worm Wormley would become the Chief of Police because his father had promised free ice-cream sundaes to the city officials at the end of their day in office; Peanuts Dunkle would be Fire Chief because he had red hair and always wore a red shirt.

Last of all, Shoie was to become City Collector. He'd been told about the appointment two days before. He would have preferred to be Chief of Police "so I can ride around in a squad car and arrest people," but Speedy had talked him into the City Collector's job.

"But I don't even know what the City Collector does," Shoie had argued when the three boys had discussed the subject.

Alvin wasn't sure either. "Maybe he collects the garbage."

"Geeeeeeek." Speedy was disgusted. "He collects tax money and turns it over to the City Treasurer."

"But nobody's going to give *me* any money that day. They'll just wait until the real Collector is back on the job."

"True," admitted Speedy. "But we have other plans for you, Shoie. Big plans. Don't we, Alvin?"

Alvin found himself saying yes without even knowing what those plans were.

Now, in the Mayor's office, Shoie walked over to take his place beside the real City Collector. As he walked in front of Speedy, some whispered words passed between the two. Alvin overheard Speedy say, "Don't forget. Get your bike and come right back." What was this all about?

But now Mayor Massey was turning back to Alvin. "Mr. Mayor, I'd like to present you with the key to the city. And may you administer this office wisely during your short term."

Mayor Massey reached into a desk drawer and pulled out a beautiful key, glistening gold, at least a foot long.

"Thank you," said Alvin. Then he added thoughtfully, "What does it unlock?"

The Mayor laughed. "I'm afraid it's only a symbol, Alvin. It means that the city is yours, for the rest of the day."

Alvin cleared his throat to begin his speech. Just then Mayor Massey said to the six men, "Take these fine youngsters to your offices, show them around, describe your duties, and leave them something to do. Good luck, kids!"

Alvin opened his mouth, the first words of his speech in his throat.

"I'll see you men on the golf course promptly at ten o'clock," said the Mayor.

"My good friends—" began Alvin.

"Don't get into any trouble, kids," said Mayor Massey as he walked around the desk and picked up his hat from the table. "The police and fire departments are on duty as always, and I'll have Miss Carner drop by later to check up on you, Alvin. There will also be one adult on duty in each of the city offices."

"But—but what about my speech?" spluttered Alvin.

"Oh?" said the Mayor, raising his eyebrows. "So you have a speech? Well, I hope it's short. People don't like politicians who give long speeches. Well, go ahead, go ahead."

"My good friends and fellow citizens of Riverton—" said Alvin, noticing that the Mayor hadn't even put down his hat.

So began Alvin Fernald's term in office as Mayor of Riverton. If he had known what was coming within a few hours, he might have resigned on the spot.

7

What About Those
Campaign Promises?

Alvin suddenly was very lonely. Seated behind the Mayor's enormous desk—*his* desk—he felt very small and helpless. He propped his elbows up on the broad polished surface and cupped his chin in his hands, holding his head up so he would appear taller. At the same time, he shifted his weight to the front of the chair, which suddenly skittered backwards on its smooth wheels. Alvin lost his balance and vanished as though a trapdoor had opened beneath him.

He got awkwardly to his feet, face reddening, and pulled the chair back over to the desk. Gingerly he sat down again. A spring squeaked softly, breaking the silence.

The only other person in the room was Speedy Glomitz, who was seated in a big leather chair. He looked at Alvin for a long moment, then got slowly to his feet, walked around behind his chair, and with considerable effort shoved it across the thick carpet until it was close to Mayor Fernald's desk. Then he dropped into it again, scrunched down, and put his feet up on the desk.

"Doggone it!" shouted Alvin. "Keep your feet off my desk! Do you want to scratch it or something? Doggone it, Speedy, I'm mad at you! Why didn't you leave with the rest of the kids?"

After Alvin had given his speech, his city officials had filed out to go to their respective offices. Alvin (at Speedy's whispered suggestion) had asked the rest of the kids to go back to the school playground and wait for a message from him, because he wanted them *all* to take part in his administration, in one way or another.

"Alvin, I reckon you don't remember your promise to me," said Speedy slowly. His feet remained on the desk. "You promised your office would always be open to me. Remember?"

"Yes—sure," spluttered Alvin. "But that doesn't mean you can *live* in here. Besides, I have important—"

Just then the door opened and the Pest poked her golden head into the room. "Al—I mean Mr. Mayor, Your Sirness! Sorry to interrupt you." She walked gaily into the room, a stenographer's pad in one hand, a pencil in the other. "I thought you might have some dictation for me."

"Doggone it, Pest, you know you can't take dictation."

"Well, I could try. I could make some of those

43

funny squiggles on the paper, like the secretaries do. Besides, I want to show you how to buzz me. Miss Carner showed me how." She walked over until she was standing beside Alvin, then reached under the edge of the desk and pressed a button. Faintly, Alvin heard a buzzer sound in the reception room. "See?" said the Pest brightly. "Just push the button and I'll come running."

"Okay, okay. Now get out."

The Pest walked out the door and slammed it behind her.

"You too, Speedy. Get out. I have to do some thinking."

Speedy remained where he was, his feet still on the desk. "What are you going to think about?" he asked softly.

"Well—well—" There was a long pause as Alvin struggled to answer. "Well, about the problems of the city, and all that kind of stuff."

"In other words, you're going to be a do-nothing mayor."

Alvin opened his mouth to reply, then closed it again when he could think of nothing to say.

"What about your campaign promises?"

Alvin was trying to think of an answer when the door burst open and the Pest leaped inside. "Your Excellency," she shouted dramatically, "Shoie—I mean Mr. Wilfred Shoemaker, your City Collector—wishes to be announced!"

Shoie shoved past her with a grin, suddenly turned a back flip on the deep carpet, and ended up sitting on the edge of the desk. "Hi, guys. What's up? How come you wanted me to leave the Collector's office, run home, get my bike, and come back here?"

Alvin picked up the fancy pitcher on the desk and poured himself a glass of water. He was struggling to keep control of the situation, but felt he was losing the battle.

"We were just talking about Alvin's campaign promises," said Speedy. "What are we going to do about them?"

"What campaign promises?" asked Alvin, stalling for time.

"Well, let's see," said Speedy. He held up a hand and began ticking off his fingers one by one. "You promised a stop sign at the corner of Maple and Third Streets, so kids could ride their bikes safely in that area. You promised to convert vacant lots into playgrounds. You promised to enforce the law against peddlers going from house to house. And you promised more convenient bus routes. Now, what are you going to do about those promises?"

"About those promises," whispered the Pest from the doorway.

"Well," said Alvin lamely. "Well, nobody can expect me to do anything in just one day."

"Why not?"

"Why not?" A whisper from the doorway again.

"Why not?" repeated Speedy. "There's no reason why not. Alvin, in the next five or six hours you can be the talk of the town *if you'll just take control*. If you'll just *be* Mayor Fernald, instead of some stuffed-shirt kid sitting behind a big desk with orange owls peeking over the edge. Oooooof. Those owls!"

"But how——" began Alvin.

"I'll tell you how. You have key kids in all the key offices in this town, just waiting for you to pick up the phone and tell them what to do. You have twenty-two other kids playing baseball and kickball over on the school grounds, eager to help you run this city. You have Shoie here, ready to carry any private messages for you on his bike, and he's the fastest bike rider in school—that's why you picked him."

"It is?" said Alvin.

"And you have my brains, to work behind the scenes."

"Don't forget me!" piped the Pest.

"You also have your sister to place phone calls for you, and do anything else you demand," said Speedy.

The Magnificent Brain began stirring into action. "You know," said Alvin thoughtfully, "we *might* be able to do something at that."

8

The Mayor Goes Into Action

"Of course we can do something about those campaign promises," said Speedy. "You promised ACTION! Let's produce it. You promised to put up a stop sign. What shall we do about that?"

"We'll put it up!" exclaimed Alvin, leaping to his feet. "Doggone it, we'll put it up, whether the quarry wants it there or not! After all, who's Mayor of this town?" He began pacing back and forth behind the desk.

"Attaboy!" shouted Shoie.

Alvin stopped in midstride. "But where will we get it?"

"We'll make it ourselves," suggested Speedy.

"Make it ourselves," echoed the Pest.

"Right!" said Alvin, his voice taking on an air of authority. Suddenly he felt wonderful. "Pest, get me Spider—I mean my Commissioner of Public Works—on the phone."

"Right away, your Majesty," said the Pest. "Before Miss Carner left, she showed me how to use the phone with all the different buttons on it. Now, when you hear the buzzer, you'll see a light flashing on your phone. You push in that button, and then you can talk." She dashed into her own office.

"What's the next item?" asked Alvin. "Doggone it, let's get some things done around here!"

"Be patient. One thing at a time."

Just then the buzzer sounded. Alvin jerked up the phone and shouted "Hello!" The line was dead. Then he remembered, and pushed in the button that was flashing.

"Hello. . . . Hello, Spider? . . . Your Mayor here, Mayor Alvin Fernald. . . . Yeah, I'm having fun too, Spide. Listen, Spide. I want you to do something for me, and do it right away. Just walk out of your office, and go on home. . . . No, wait, Spider! You aren't fired! This is in the line of duty. I named you Commissioner of Public Works, and I expect action out of you. Don't tell any adults that might be around there what you're doing. Just go on home as fast as you can, find a big board, and nail a pointy board onto it. You're making a sign, see? The pointy board is to stick in the ground. Make the sign as big as you can. Wait a minute, Spide, I'll be right back."

Speedy was gesturing wildly at Alvin. In his hand he held a piece of paper. "Have Spider print this on the sign," he said.

On the paper were the words: *Stop! No More Bike Accidents Here. Please. The Kids of Riverton.*

Alvin was puzzled, but he started talking into the phone again. "Listen, Spide. After you get the sign built—and do it in a hurry—find some bright red paint in your dad's workshop. You got a pencil and paper handy? Right. Now print this in big letters on the sign." Alvin read him the lettering on the slip of paper.

"Now listen, Spider. When you finish lettering it, take it over to the corner of Maple and Third Streets. There'll be a couple of kids from our class waiting for you over there, and they'll help you pound it in the ground."

At that point there was a lot of static from the phone, and Alvin held it away from his ear. For some reason his heart was pounding and the Magnificent Brain was lighting up like a switchboard. The static gradually died down.

"Yeah, Spide. I know. Don't worry, I'll take full responsibility. You just go ahead and do it, like a good Commissioner of Public Works, and if anybody complains, just tell them to call the Mayor's office. Okay? . . . Listen, Spide, get that sign up, and then watch for a while and see what happens. Then call me back. . . . Yeah, Spide, I won't forget about the ice cream sundae."

Alvin slammed down the phone with authority. He still held the slip of paper in his hand. "How come you thought we should put this lettering on the sign?" he asked Speedy.

"Public opinion. It can do almost anything in a town this size." Speedy got to his feet and poured

50

himself a drink out of the fancy water jug. "Wait and see. Every driver that comes to that intersection will stop to read the sign. And most drivers will remember the girl who was killed there last year. Pretty soon one of those drivers will call the *Daily Bugle* and say he thinks the sign is a good idea. The *Bugle* will send a photographer to take pictures of it. Pictures appear in paper. Phone calls from citizens. Publicity. Strong public reaction. The quarry won't dare fight it then. You'll see." He gulped down the water.

Alvin admired the logic. "Okay," he said. "Shoie, you're City Collector. You ride on over to the school yard, and collect a couple of the kids. Tell them to meet Spider at Maple and Third, and help him put up the sign."

As Shoie leaped for the door, Speedy suddenly said, "Wait!" Shoie spun on one foot and came back toward the desk.

"Let's not waste Shoie's time," said Speedy quietly. "Let's look at Campaign Promise Number Two before he goes. What are we going to do about building playgrounds on the vacant lots?"

"We'll do it!" exclaimed Alvin, caught up in his own enthusiasm. When neither of the boys said anything, Alvin sat back down at the desk and cupped his chin in his hands. "But how?"

"We'll just *do* it," replied Speedy.

"But those vacant lots don't really belong to the city. We'd have to get permission."

51

"And who gives permits to do most things around town?"

"The City Clerk." As soon as he said it, the beautiful simplicity of it struck Alvin, and he jammed his finger against the buzzer.

Instantly the door flew open. Alvin knew the Pest had been waiting just outside.

"Call my City Clerk," ordered Alvin.

"Right away, Your Sirship," answered the Pest. Then her lower lip went out. "Alvin, I never do know exactly what to call you."

"Just call me my City Clerk, like I asked you," Alvin said with a grin.

A moment later the light flashed on the base of the phone. Alvin snatched up the receiver. "Hello, Hortense? Mayor Fernald here. . . . Okay, I know there hasn't been much for you to do so far, but listen. I want you to write out two permits for me. One for the vacant lot on Myrtle Street, the other for that one over by the old warehouse. I want permits to make 'em into playgrounds. . . . Yeah, Hortense, I *know* you don't know how to write permits. Just listen and I'll tell you. Got a pencil? Okay, just say something like, 'I hereby give the kids of Riverton permission to make a playground at—' and so on. And then sign your name, and under it write City Clerk. . . . No, Hortense, you won't get in any trouble. Just slip those two permits into the files where they keep the other permits— just in case. And listen, Hortense. Keep this under your hat if there are any adults around."

Alvin slammed down the phone and looked at the other two boys, grinning. "Okay, now we have permission to do anything we want with those two lots. You know, I'm getting to like this job. Now that we have permission, how are we going to change those weedy lots into playgrounds?"

Speedy settled deeper into the leather chair. "Mayor, you have twenty-two kids over at the schoolgrounds just awaiting your orders."

The Magnificent Brain slipped smoothly into action. "Okay, Shoie, you ride on over to the playground. Chase two of the guys over to help Spider with the stop sign. Then divide all the rest of the kids into two groups. Put somebody in charge of each group that has some sense. I know it's hard to find somebody like that, but *do* it. Have all the kids go home and get their lawnmowers, rakes, and shovels, and tell them to get to work cleaning up those vacant lots."

"But that's no fun," said Shoie. "They won't want to do it."

"Well. . . . Well. . . ." Finally Alvin said in desperation. "Tell them they can all join us for sundaes at Wormley's Ice Cream Shoppe tonight."

"Geez! They'll go for that!"

"Listen a minute," said Speedy. "Haaaaaaarrf. We don't want people to think we're just building baseball diamonds for our own use. They might not like it. It sounds pretty selfish."

Alvin thought a minute. "You're right. Tell you what you do, Shoie. Send a few of the girls scrounging around for some old swing sets and slides that people leave in their back yards after their kids have outgrown them. As soon as they've spotted four or five, have the girls offer to haul them away. Then have some of the bigger boys take them over to that vacant lot on Myrtle. We'll make that into a playground for little kids. We might even put in a sandbox there, if we have time. We'll make the lot over by the old warehouse into a baseball and kickball field. Now, get going! Collect all those kids, City Collector!"

After Shoie slammed the door, Alvin looked across at Speedy. Instead of resenting Speedy, he was beginning to be glad he was there.

Suddenly a thought troubled him. This time he looked to Speedy for help. "Speedy, why'd I promise all that free ice cream to the rest of the kids? Where am I going to get the money to pay for it?"

"Poooooooooot," said Speedy, exhaling as he thought over the problem. "Look, Alvin, we don't have to solve all these problems ourselves. You need money. Now, I ask you, who handles all the money in this town?"

"Well . . . the City Treasurer, I guess."

"Why not pitch the problem to Alicia? She's *your* City Treasurer."

"Speedy!" said Alvin in horror. "We couldn't steal the money from the city treasury."

"I didn't say anything about stealing. Just tell her how much you need, and ask her to get it. She's got a lot of imagination. She'll find a way, and she'll do it honestly."

Alvin did some quick arithmetic, then had the Pest call his City Treasurer. "Hello, Alicia? Mayor Fernald speaking. Listen, I need nine dollars and thirty-six cents, including tax, by the end of the day. It's for a good cause—you might even say for civic improvement. Alicia, I want you, as City Treasurer, to get us that money. I don't care how you do it, as long as you do it honestly. Now, get to work on it."

He hung up before she had a chance to answer.

9

A Mysterious Leatherbound Book

The Magnificent Brain suddenly was tired, and its circuits only lighted up with weak flashes.

Mayor Fernald had been operating at full speed all morning. With Speedy's help (sometimes to Alvin it seemed the other way around) he had been "ruling the city of Riverton" and also keeping tabs on all the kids of Miss Pinkney's Fifth Grade class, Room 3B, Roosevelt School.

By now, Spider should be putting up his homemade stop sign. By now, most of the kids should be cleaning up the two vacant lots. By now, Alicia should have solved the problem of digging up $9.36, including tax.

All these arrangements had taken so much time that Mayor Fernald hadn't been able to inspect the city offices, as he had planned, or check up personally on the work of his appointed officials. The time had gone so fast that he didn't realize it was noon until his stomach growled.

At that moment one of the lights flashed on the phone. Mayor Fernald sighed. It certainly wasn't easy being Mayor of a city the size of Riverton.

"Mayor Fernald speaking."

"Hello, Alvin? I m-m-m-m-mean Mayor Fernald? This is Worm, your Chief of Police."

"Yeah, Worm. I could have guessed who it was. What's the problem?"

"No p-p-p-p-p-problem, Alvin. I just wanted to tell you something."

"Okay, Worm. Tell me, but just take it easy. Speak very slowly, like Miss Pinkney taught you." Worm hardly stammered at all, except when he was excited.

"Yeah, Alvin, I'll talk real slow. Alvin, the Police Headquarters is n-n-neat. I just thought you might like to know. And your father, who's on duty over here while the Chief is playing golf, has been treating me g-great."

"Good. Anything else, Worm?"

"Well, no. Just thought you'd like to know. Your father just showed me how the police c-c-contact the FBI if they want to find out anything about anybody. There's a machine here that looks like a typewriter, only it's connected to FBI headquarters. You just type out what you want to know, and pretty soon the typewriter starts writing all by itself, and types out an answer. It's g-g-great!"

"Glad you like it, Worm. Anything else going on down there?"

"Not much. There's a report that some house-to-house peddlers are operating on the east side of town."

A bell rang in the back of Alvin's mind. House-to-house peddlers. Another of his campaign promises.

"Listen, Worm, are the police doing anything about those peddlers?"

"No. They say Mayor Massey has given orders that any p-p-peddlers are to go to his office. He sometimes lets them operate in town, even though it's against the law. I think it makes the police kind of mad that he handles it himself."

Alvin thought for a moment. "Okay, Worm. Let me know anything else you hear."

"Okay, Mayor. S-s-so long."

As soon as Alvin hung up, the door opened and the Pest skipped in. "Guess what, Alvin. Antonio's Pizza Parlor just delivered a big package. There's a note on it that says, 'Lunch for the Mayor's office, with Antonio's compliments.'"

"Great. Bring it in."

"Wait." The voice was Speedy's. "Look, Alvin. When you're Mayor, or President, or anything, people try to give you presents so *you'll* do favors for *them*. Maybe we'd better not eat that pizza."

"But I'm hungry. Besides, what could I do for Antonio's Pizza Parlor?"

"I dunno."

Alvin thought for a moment. The smell of pizza was drifting in from the reception room. "Pest, get the owner of Antonio's on the phone. I think I'll talk to him."

A moment later he was saying, "Hello, Mr. Antonio? Look, this is Mayor Fernald. Thanks a lot for the lunch you sent over. It smells mighty good. . . . Look, just one more thing. You don't expect me to do anything in return do you? I mean, I'm Mayor, and I wouldn't want to eat the pizza if you wanted me to—"

Alvin held the receiver away from his ear so the other kids could hear the friendly laughter from the other end. Then he listened for a moment longer. "Just sent it out of respect for the new Mayor, huh? Well, thanks Mr. Antonio. That was mighty nice of you. Goodby." He put down the receiver. "Pest, bring in that package immediately."

When the Pest had lunch laid out on the desk, the kids were awestruck. There were ten pizzas, one of each type that Antonio's served. They were all the huge family size, so they not only overlapped the top of the Mayor's desk but overflowed to the coffee table.

For several minutes no one said a word. The kids ate on their feet, roaming around the big desk, and drifting over to the coffee table so they could sample everything. Still, they could hardly see where they had touched that vast blanket of pizza.

Finally, still nibbling, Alvin sat down at the desk. "Might as well do a little city business while we're eating," he said between bites. "A Mayor's job is never done." He sighed, looking for sympathy.

When he got none, he said, "Speedy, how many more campaign promises did we make?"

"Two." Speedy swallowed a mouthful of pepperoni pizza. "Get rid of the peddlers, and improve the bus routes."

"Well, I've got an idea on the peddlers," said Alvin. "But I want it to cook in the old M.B. for a while." That's what Alvin sometimes called his Magnificent Brain. "Meanwhile, let's see what we can do about the bus routes. How come you promised to add some new bus routes in my campaign speech, Speedy?"

The other boy swallowed a final bite of pizza and patted his stomach. Then, as he thought about Alvin's question, a rather sheepish look crossed his face. It somehow didn't fit Speedy's personality, for Speedy always seemed so sure of himself.

"Well, if you really want to know, I only wanted to add one new route. And I suggested that because of old Mrs. Toomey. You know her—she lives over on Highland Avenue. Her husband has been in the hospital for more than six months now, and she goes to see him every day. But there's no bus route close by, so she has to walk about half a mile to catch the bus. I see her limping along on her cane on my way to school." He paused, then added lamely, "I'll admit that's not much of a reason to add a new bus route—just for one old lady."

Alvin gazed at him steadily, thinking it over. Finally he said, "I think it's a fine reason, Speedy.

Besides, if she has trouble catching a bus, so does everyone who lives near her."

"That's true, I suppose."

"Well, how do we go about adding a new bus route?"

"I don't really know, Alvin. I had some ideas on your other campaign promises, but not this one. But it doesn't seem like it should be too hard, just to add one new bus route. After all, the bus system is owned by the city. Seems like the Mayor ought to be able to make changes if he wants to."

"Maybe if we just filled out some kind of form, and sent it over to the bus line headquarters, it would work."

"I doubt it," said Speedy, "but it's worth a try. I'll bet there's a regular form that's used for the purpose."

"Hey, Pest," said Alvin. "Stop eating that anchovy and sausage pizza, and get to work. Look through the filing cabinets, and see if you can find some kind of form for changing the bus routes."

"Right away, Your Excellency."

The Pest skipped over to the file cabinets and pulled out the drawer marked "B" for Bus. When she couldn't find anything there, she tried "C" for Changing Bus Routes. She was just looking under "W" for What If the Mayor Wants to Change Bus Routes when Shoie burst through the door.

"You shoulda seen what hap—" His eyes fell on the vast remains of the pizzas, spread like a tattered sheet across the desk. "Geez, you guys really live it up while us peasants are out there working!"

"Help yourself, old man," said Alvin. "What did you start to say?"

A big grin spread across Shoie's face. "You shoulda seen what happened over at Maple and Third Street. Ole Spider, he got hold of a board about as big as a barn door, and painted the sign like you said. He's not a very good printer, but the letters are so big nobody could miss them. He and the other two kids finally got the sign pounded into the ground. Right away, drivers started slamming on their brakes to read the sign. Most of them grinned and waved at us before they drove off. Pretty soon, all the little kids in the neighborhood were kind of clustered around and shouting, and betting each other whether the next car would stop.

"Anyway, pretty soon a police car came cruising by, and the officer who was driving slammed on his brakes, too. Then he hollered over to us and asked who was responsible for the sign. Spider was pretty scared, but he went over to the car and said he was Commissioner of Public Works, and was just following the orders of the Mayor. For a minute the officer looked kind of stern, then he started smiling, then he let out with a big laugh. He didn't say a thing, just drove away. I suppose he thinks they'll wait till the end of the day and then just take the sign down.

"Then along came a truck from the quarry. The driver was the most surprised guy in the world, and hit his brakes so hard part of his load of gravel slurped out of the truck. We helped him clean it up.

"As soon as he drove away, here comes a man from the *Daily Bugle* with five cameras hanging around his neck. He took about two dozen pictures of that sign. He had Spider pose with it, then all the kids that were hanging around pose with it, especially those with bicycles. He got some red paint on his jacket, but when he left he said to be sure to look in the paper tonight."

"Great!" said Speedy, rubbing his hands together. "That's exactly what we want—publicity."

"Good work," said Mayor Fernald crisply. "That's what I like—real action from my staff. After all, we're in charge of this town. Now, how about the playgrounds?"

"Man, you should have seen all those kids go to work when I told them you promised them an ice cream sundae tonight. I think they kind of like the job anyway, even though they'd moan about that kind of work at home. They've got both vacant lots pretty well cleaned up already, and now they're shoveling dirt around to level them off. A couple of the kids are starting to build baseball bases out of old gunny sacks, and on the little kids' playground we've already got three old swing sets dug into the ground, and some preschool kids are playing on them."

The Pest had given up on the filing cabinets, and had disappeared into her office. Now she skipped back into the room.

"Al—I mean Your Highness," she said, "I thought maybe Miss Carner kept the forms for the bus route in her office, so I began looking through her desk. I didn't find any forms, but way down in the bottom of one drawer, under a lot of stationery, I found this little book. What do you suppose it is?"

Alvin took the little leatherbound book and opened it. At first it didn't make much sense. He started reading aloud a long list of names: "Buskin Black Dirt Company, Arrow Magazine Subscription Company, Magnetic Furnace Examiners, Holiday Landscaping Service. . . ."

"I don't get it," said Shoie.

"Wait a minute!" There was a note of urgency in Speedy's voice. "Is there anything except a list of names there, Alvin?"

"After each name there's a date, starting about a year ago, followed by an amount of money, from twenty-five dollars to, let's see"—he riffled through the pages quickly—"three hundred dollars."

Speedy suddenly was sitting straight up in his chair, which was something Alvin had never seen him do before. "I'll bet I know what that is, but I sure hope I'm wrong!"

"What?" asked the Mayor and the City Collector simultaneously.

"What?" echoed the Mayor's private secretary.

"If I'm right about that book, then our Mayor is a crook. Oh, not you Alvin—I'm talking about Mayor Massey. I remember the Buskin Black Dirt Company because I happened to be home when they came around door to door. A couple of big scroungy-looking men knocked on our door. There was a truck loaded with dirt out front. They'd already spread a couple of bushels of stuff on the lawn before they knocked. When Mom opened the door and said she didn't want any, one of them got his toe in the door and said she owed him for the dirt he'd already spread. Pretty soon Mom was arguing with them, and threatening to call the police. The man who was doing the talking said, 'Fat lot of good that will do you, lady. The police won't do a thing.' Then he kind of smiled an ugly smile at her, as though he knew something she didn't. To tell the truth, I was kinda scared. Anyway, she argued so much that they finally left. It wasn't very good dirt anyway."

"What's that go to do with this list?" asked Alvin.

"Don't you see? The Buskin Black Dirt Company is on this list. There's a law against house-to-house peddling in this town, but the Mayor has ordered the police not to enforce it. Instead, the peddler always has to come to the Mayor's office. Here, as we say in politics, the Mayor puts the bite on him. For a certain amount of money, the Mayor lets him operate in Riverton. This is a list, for the Mayor's eyes alone, of the amount of money he's collected in the past year. Is there a total there, Alvin?"

"Let's see. Yeah. After the final entry it says twelve thousand, seven hundred and fifty dollars. Wow! That much money in just one year! And I'm worried about digging up nine dollars and thirty-six cents, including tax!"

Something was deeply troubling the Pest. "But if I found this in Miss Carner's desk, then it means—" She hated to put her thoughts into words. Finally the words tumbled out. "It means she knows all about it, and that makes her a crook, too!"

"Dad said the Mayor brought her here, from out of town, after he was elected," said Alvin thoughtfully.

There was a long silence in the room. Finally Shoie broke it. "What are we going to do, Alvin?"

10

A Difference in Dimensions

The Magnificent Brain clicked. Mayor Fernald sat up straight in his chair and took command. "I'll tell you what we're going to do. All we have so far is a little book full of suspicions."

Without thinking, he slapped the book down on the desk. Bits of sausage and tomato sauce flew across the room. "We're going to see if we can find more proof before we make any accusations. That's only fair. Meanwhile, Shoie, I want you to ride across town and find Evil Eye Davis."

Evil Eye Davis!

Just the name was enough to stun any kid in town. Evil Eye, the ultimate weapon, the most dangerous person in Riverton! He was only a third-grader—Willy Davis' little brother—but he was already one of the most famous kids in town. It was unbelievable what he could do, alone and with no weapon in his hands.

Alvin knew that Evil Eye had discovered his

strange talent in kindergarten. The kindergarten teacher hadn't returned to school the following year. Alvin was aware that she had been married during the summer, but most of the kids said she had done it as a last resort, so she wouldn't have to be in the same school with Evil Eye for another year.

Evil Eye had a strange weapon. He leaned his head to one side and speared his victim with his eyes. It reminded Alvin of the summer he had collected butterflies, and pinned them to a board on the wall of his room. Evil Eye's gaze was like that —so sharp and steady that his victim seemed helpless. Those two eyes stared out through the bright red hair that tumbled down across his forehead. Strangest of all, there was no expression on his face. When Evil Eye was doing his act, Alvin had never seen him smile or even blink. Threats, anger, laughter—nothing ever changed his face.

Even if his victim was an older and larger kid, it made no difference to Evil Eye. The victim soon began to get mad, then nervous, then desperate under Evil Eye's spell. Once Alvin had seen Evil Eye force Mr. Simpson to drop a gallon of paint from the top of an extension ladder. Another time, Alvin himself had been the victim, stopped dead by Evil Eye from all the way across the street.

All the kids loved to watch Evil Eye operate on someone else, but when he turned his attention to *you* it was downright terrifying.

"Pick up Evil Eye," ordered Mayor Fernald, "and then go over to the playground and get a couple of the bigger boys from our class. All of you head for the east side of town and find the peddlers that are operating there this afternoon. Have Evil Eye put his spell on them. I can't think of any way to drive them out of town any faster."

"Beautiful," said Shoie. He dragged out each syllable.

"Beautiful," echoed the Pest. She'd been Evil Eye's victim just once.

"Listen, Shoie." Alvin grew very serious. "You three older boys are there to protect Evil Eye. Don't let him get too close to the men—he operates mighty good from a distance—and keep your bikes handy. *Don't get in any trouble!* If the men start threatening you, hop on your bikes and ride away."

"Yes, *sir!*" Shoie started for the door, relishing the assignment.

"And let me know what happens!"

The door slammed shut.

Alvin looked up at Speedy and the Pest. "I suppose you know what we're going to do now?"

Speedy nodded. The boys were beginning to work so well together that they could read each other's minds.

"Speedy, you take the file cabinets. Pest, you continue to search Miss Carner's desk. And I'll take the Mayor's desk. Look for anything suspicious. It's not a nice thing to do, searching someone's desk, but if the Mayor is cheating the town, I think the citizens ought to know about it."

Thirty minutes later, as they were about to give

up, Alvin reached into the very back of the bottom drawer of the Mayor's desk. His fingers brushed across the edge of a sheet of paper, then came back, grabbed the corner, and tugged. Out it came. It was an ordinary sheet of white paper, with a lot of figures scrawled on it in pencil, and what appeared to be the rough floor plan of a building. It didn't make sense, and he was about to slip it back into the drawer when he suddenly noticed Speedy looking over his shoulder.

"Probably nothing important," said Alvin.

"Wait. Let's take another look. There's something familiar about that floor plan."

Alvin moved the cold pepperoni pizza over on top of the cold anchovy pizza to make room on the desk. Both boys gazed thoughtfully at the sheet of paper.

"That appears to be the foundation plan for a building," said Speedy.

"Might be. Sort of shaped like a U. Any buildings around here shaped like that?"

"Not that I can think of."

The Magnificent Brain took over. "Wait. Let's analyze this scientifically." It was one of the M.B.'s favorite phrases. "If this is a foundation plan, it's probably for a fairly new building, or one that's just being built. Does that get us anywhere?"

A split second later, both boys solved the puzzle at the same time. "The new City Hall!" they shouted in unison. The Pest came running in to see what had happened.

"Look," said Alvin, "it's the same shape as the City Hall. We didn't recognize it at first because all they've done so far is pour the foundation, so it's kind of hard to visualize the shape."

"Visualize the shape," said the Pest. "But what does it mean, Al—I mean Your Most Sirness?"

Speedy was gazing intently at the paper. "See? You can see the foundation sketched in by these two lines. But between them there's a dotted line all around the foundation. Do you suppose that means anything?"

"And what about these figures?" said Alvin. He analyzed them carefully. "The figure twenty-four appears lots of times at first, then the figure eighteen sort of takes over toward the bottom of the page."

The puzzle had only deepened. The Magnificent Brain took over again. "Once more, scientifically. We've already figured out that this is a sketch of the foundation for the new City Hall, which the Mayor has been determined to build since he took office. Now, what could the numbers twenty-four and eighteen mean on a building plan?" He looked up at Speedy.

Suddenly Speedy's normally sleepy eyes flew open. It was a truly remarkable sight, for Alvin had never seen the tops of Speedy's eyeballs before.

"I think I've got it, Alvin!" said Speedy in a low, tense voice. "It's a change in dimensions for the building."

"What kind of dimensions?"

"See? Here's the foundation plan. And here's a

dotted line, as though the Mayor was thinking about making a change. And the dotted line makes the foundation *narrower*. It should be twenty-four inches thick, all around. But this dotted line makes it eighteen inches thick."

Mayor Fernald thought for a moment. Suddenly he ripped off the orange-owl tie and unbuttoned his collar. Things were getting a little warm.

"Wow!" he exclaimed. "Think of all the concrete that would save."

"Right. Now look at this figure down at the bottom. It says, 'M.C.C. Twelve thousand dollars.' "

"M.C.C." Alvin was growing more excited. "I'll bet that means Markle Construction Company. They're building the new City Hall. Remember? The Mayor said nobody in town was qualified to build that big a building, and insisted on bringing in the Markle Company from out of town. A lot of people didn't like it at the time, but the Mayor had his way."

"And the twelve thousand dollars?" asked Speedy in a whisper.

Both boys knew what it meant, or at least thought they did. Neither wanted to put it into words.

Finally Alvin managed to say it. "Mayor Massey changed the width of the foundation from twenty-four inches to eighteen inches. Nobody pays much attention to a foundation when it's going in, and pretty soon it's all covered up. He saved the Markle Company a lot of money in concrete. And in return, he gets twelve thousand dollars from the Markle Company without anybody knowing about it."

"A kickback," said Speedy.

"A kickback," echoed the Pest. She'd never heard the word before, but suddenly she knew what it meant.

Mayor Fernald stood up. "That might make the building unsafe," he said.

"What are we going to do?" asked Speedy.

The question bothered Alvin. Speedy had always seemed to *know* what to do, seemed so sure of himself. Now, when they had uncovered something serious, Speedy was at a loss.

"We could tell Daddy," suggested the Pest.

"Slow down," said Mayor Fernald. "We *think* the Mayor has been taking money behind the scenes from the peddlers. And we *think* he's taking a big kickback on the construction of City Hall. *But we still don't have positive proof.* Just suspicions. The first thing to do is try to get proof. Pest, get me my Commissioner of Public Works on the phone."

"Right away, Your Greatship."

As soon as the phone call went through, Alvin said, "Hello, Spider? . . . Yeah, you did a great job on that stop sign. . . . You've been interviewed by a reporter? . . . Hey, that's great. Look, Spider, I have another job for you. Do you see any plans around the office there, plans for the new City Hall? . . . Lots of them, all over the place? Good. Spider, here's what I wish you'd do. Look at a set of those plans, and see if you can find the sheet that shows the foundation. It'll probably be the sheet right on top. I'll wait. . . . Got it, Spide? Good. Look, I know you're not an engineer, but look all over that sheet and see if you can find out how thick the foundation is supposed to be. . . . Yeah, I'll wait some more."

Alvin managed to shrug out of his sport coat while still holding the receiver. "Got it, Spide? The plan says the foundation is supposed to be twenty-four inches thick? Okay. Now, find a ruler there in the office, and run on over to the new City Hall. *Measure* the foundation, right on the spot, and then call me back. And Spider—maybe you'd better not say anything to anyone about this."

They waited a long five minutes before the phone rang. Alvin leaped for it. "The Mayor here. . . . Yeah, Spider, of course it's me, Alvin. What did you find out? . . . You're sure? . . . Okay. Don't say anything to anybody about this. And thanks, Spide."

He hung up the phone. There was absolute silence in the room.

Finally Alvin said in a low voice, as though to no one in particular, "The foundation measures only eighteen inches thick."

11

A Message to the FBI

"Well," said Mayor Fernald, seated at his desk. He tugged at his left ear, which he frequently did when he was nervous. "Well, what are we going to do?"

"Let's tell Daddy," said the Pest in a tiny voice.

Speedy shifted uncomfortably in his chair. "Urrrmmmm. Alvin, I'm kind of scared. We've done some pretty good things—together—since you became Mayor. I suppose we can be proud of ourselves. But this is something different." He flushed. "I'm resigning. This is pretty serious, and I'm leaving." He stood up and started for the door.

Alvin had a sinking feeling, as though he'd been betrayed. "Wait a minute, Speedy. We did some pretty good things all right, and most of them were your ideas. If it hadn't been for you, I'd still be sitting at this fancy desk wondering what to do. I *thought* I was a big shot, but I really wasn't. You made me *do* things like a big shot. Now, sit down and tell me once more what to do. If things go wrong, it will be my fault, but I need your help. Besides, you can't resign. I never appointed you to anything."

Speedy turned and shuffled back to the chair, a slightly shamed look on his face. "Well. . . . Okay, Alvin. . . . I guess we've both learned something today. You're full of big ideas, and will take responsibility for them, but you don't know how to carry them out. I know how to manage kids—sort of move them around behind the scenes, so they'll do what we want—but to tell the truth I'm scared silly, now that we've found something really serious."

"I *still* need your help. Now let's think about this scientifically. We think the Mayor is taking money from peddlers, and then letting them break the law. We have no proof. We think the Mayor is taking a big wad of money by cheating on the construction of City Hall. We have no proof."

"But we *do* have proof," piped up the Pest. "That piece of paper on your desk."

"That isn't proof. Maybe there really is an honest change in the building plans, a change Mayor Massey is making that will save the taxpayers money. And he was just figuring out how *much* it will save the taxpayers. We'd look pretty silly if that was the case."

Speedy had thrown his legs over the arm of the chair again. He pillowed his head on the other arm and stared at the ceiling. "Look," he said, his forehead wrinkled in thought, "suppose you suspect a person of being a crook. If he's a criminal right now, it's very likely he's been a criminal before. Now, where do you go to find out if he has a record?"

"I could go over to the post office," offered the Pest, "and see if his picture's over there. They show pictures of lots of criminals on the bulletin board."

"No, no," said Alvin to his little sister. "If his picture appeared over there, everybody in town would know about it. To answer your question, Speedy, you'd go to the police to find out if a man has a criminal record."

"And suppose there wasn't any record listed at police headquarters—as there wouldn't be in this case. Then where would the police go to find out about the man?"

After a moment's thought, Alvin said, "The FBI."

"Right. Now if Mayor Massey has any kind of record, the FBI would know about it. We've got to ask the FBI about him."

"Let's tell Daddy. He'll know exactly how to do it."

"Wait a minute," said Alvin. "We got into this by ourselves, and all we have so far is suspicion. I don't like to tell *any* adult about it yet, even Dad. Let me think for a minute."

Now that his stomach was filled with pizza, the Magnificent Brain slipped smoothly and swiftly into operation. At least a dozen wild ideas flashed through the computer, and Alvin discarded them one by one. Then suddenly he leaped to his feet.

"I've got it!" he shouted. "I've got it!"

"What?" said Speedy.

"Follow me!" Alvin didn't even bother to put on his owly tie or his sport jacket as he ran for the door, the other two racing after him.

He dashed through the reception room, and out into the long, wide corridor. He ran down the corridor, and skidded six feet to a stop just in front of the stairway leading to the first floor. Half a dozen people who were in the corridor watched in astonishment.

It was a curved stairway, and he jumped onto the polished brass railing and slid all the way to the lower floor. He'd been doing it since he was five years old, whenever he would come to visit his father at police headquarters. Alvin raced toward the familiar door and burst in.

Sergeant Milhaus looked up in astonishment at the young man who stood in front of him, shirttail out, panting for breath.

Alvin suddenly realized *who* he was—at least for this one day—and took a deep breath just as the other two kids burst through the door behind him.

"I'm Mayor Fernald," he said, "and I'm here to talk to my Police Chief, Worm Wormley."

"Yes, Mr. Mayor," said Sergeant Milhaus with a broad grin. "You'll find him in the back room. And incidentally, Alvin, your dad's out on a routine call about a dog running around loose."

"Thank you, Sergeant." He walked as solemnly as he could behind the desk and into a small room. Worm was there alone, seated in front of a type-

writer. He looked up when he heard the door open. "Oh, hi Alvin. I m-m-m-mean, Mr. Mayor."

"Hi, Worm." Alvin closed the door carefully. "How are things going?"

"Pretty good. I like to watch this thing. They call it a t-t-t-teletype."

"Slow down, Worm. Keep your cool." Alvin had heard older kids use this expression, so he used it whenever it seemed suitable. "That's what I came to see you about, Worm. How does it work?"

"Well, you just stand there and watch. Pretty soon it will g-g-go into action. It writes out messages all by itself, whenever somebody on the other end of the line presses t-t-typewriter keys."

"And you send messages out, just by typing them?"

"Yup."

Just then the machine sprang into action. At a furious rate the keys clacked against a sheet of yellow paper running off a big roller, and the carriage moved back and forth. Suddenly there was silence.

Worm reached out a hand and ripped the message out of the machine. "See?" He looked at it. "This is a message about a stolen car that crossed into this state. Important business. I've got to give this to Sergeant Milhaus. That's why I'm here alone —to watch all these important messages come in and give them to the Sergeant. Then my police force goes into action. We'll find that c-c-c-car!"

81

Dramatically he flung open the door and disappeared.

Alvin eyed the machine in speculation.

When Worm had returned and closed the door again, Alvin said, "Worm, do you suppose you could type out a message on that machine?"

"Nope. Official business only."

"Well, suppose the message *is* official business?"

Worm thought for a minute. "I suppose I c-c-could. But why not just ask Sergeant Milhaus to do it?"

"Let's not bother him, Worm. After all, you *are* the Chief of Police."

Alvin picked up a pencil from a nearby desk, licked the point while he thought, then started writing. When he finished, he read the message aloud:

"To the FBI. Request any information past record of Melbourne Massey. Last known to be in Midwest. Six foot two, eyes of blue. Riverton Police Department."

Worm turned white when he heard the message. "Alvin, I can't send that!"

"Listen, Worm, we're going to let you in on a secret. It's a very big secret, and I don't want you to breathe a word of it. Swear?"

Worm gulped, and nodded.

The kids quickly filled him in on everything they had learned—or at least suspected—about Mayor Massey, interrupting each other in their excitement. When they'd finished, Worm gave a low whistle.

"Worm, you're my Chief of Police, so I'm going

to give you a chance to send that message. But if you don't send it, I'm going to send it myself. Okay?"

Worm nodded his head. He thought for a long moment. Then he pulled back his shoulders and lifted his head. He stood so proud that a shiver ran up Alvin's back, and he could almost hear the bugles blowing in the background, like the exciting part of a good movie. "G-g-g-give me that message!" Worm said in a voice filled with cold determination. "I'm the Chief of Police around here, and I'll send that message even if I go to p-p-p-prison for it!"

He sat down in front of the machine and flicked a switch. Then, with one finger, he began to tap out the message. It took him a good three minutes, and he misspelled two words. By the time he flicked off the switch his fingers were trembling.

Almost immediately the machine began clacking out a reply:

REQUEST WHETHER UNAUTHORIZED PERSON USING OPEN LINE TO THIS HEADQUARTERS. MESSAGE RECEIVED SLIGHTLY GARBLED BUT UNDERSTANDABLE. WHO IS TRANSMITTER?

The machine came to a stop.

Worm had been reading the message as it came in. He ripped it off the roll of paper, flicked the switch, and began typing with one finger:

CHIEF OF RIVERTON POLICE HERE. OBVIOUSLY AUTHORIZED. REQUEST PROMPT ANSWER TO

PREVIOUS MESSAGE. URGENT. CHIEF OF P-P-P-POLICE.

He looked up apologetically. "Doggone it, I even stutter on the t-t-t-teletype, but my finger stuck."

"You did fine," said Alvin. "You stay here and watch for a reply. It'll take them a little while to find out about Mayor Massey. As soon as a reply comes in, don't show it to anybody, but come right up to the Mayor's office with it."

"Yes, sir!" said Chief of Police Wormley, snapping to attention.

12

Discovered!

Upstairs, heading down the corridor toward his office, Alvin said, "About all we can do now is wait."

Suddenly he froze, and motioned frantically for the other kids to stop behind him. They'd left the office door closed, and now it was open. And they could hear voices coming from inside.

Alvin put a finger to his lips and crept closer, until he could hear the voices clearly. A man and a woman were arguing.

"I tell you I gave the Mayor one hundred and twenty-five dollars," said the man urgently. "You should know. You were right here, and accepted the money for him. In return, I was supposed to be able to pick this town clean, door to door, without any interference."

"Keep your voice down, Mr. Bates." It was Miss Carner, Mayor Massey's secretary, and her voice was just above a whisper. "I don't understand. You say some kids have been bothering you. How can kids interfere?"

"You wouldn't understand unless you were there. There's this little kid, see, about so big, and he's got a big batch of red hair. He follows me around wherever I go. And he just stands there, looking at me, with a strange kind of eye, like he was putting a spell on me. I tell you, it's weird!"

"But can't you ignore him?"

"Lady, I'd like to see you try to ignore him! He doesn't have any expression at all—he's just like a robot. And whenever any other kids see him, they start hooting and hollering and following along. Lady, I had twenty-five, maybe thirty kids following me from door to door before I finally gave up. How can you sell anything under conditions like that?"

"But can't you scare the little boy away?"

"I tried that as soon as he appeared, but there were three bigger kids who just rode past on their bikes and swept him up between them. Couple of minutes later he was right back again. Besides, can you imagine what kind of trouble I'd be in if I really took a swat at him?" He sighed. "I tell you it's weird, absolutely weird, what that little kid can do, just by staring at you. Lady, I haven't been so nervous since the last time I was picked up and thrown in jail. I'm still sweating!"

"Mr. Bates, there's really nothing I can do about it today. The Mayor is playing golf. It's an annual party, and he can't be disturbed. But I'll tell him about it later. You stop by first thing Monday, and I'm sure this can be straightened out." There was a moment's pause. "But I just can't see how one little boy can upset you so much."

"Lady, I wish that kid would start staring at *you.*"

There were sounds of rapid footsteps, then a big man, mopping his face with a handkerchief, came striding through the door. He glared at Alvin, then walked rapidly down the corridor.

Alvin thought for a moment. He whispered to the others, "Well, now we know we're right. But in front of Miss Carner we've got to pretend that nothing is wrong. Follow me."

He walked through the door, then glanced over at her as though in surprise. "Oh, hi, Miss Carner. Surprised to see you here. I thought you were taking the day off."

"Oh, I'm taking the day off all right, Mayor Fernald." A set smile moved across her face. "But Mayor Massey asked me to stop in this afternoon and check up on you. Just to make sure that everything is all right."

Everything is all wrong, thought Alvin. But he said aloud, as he walked toward the door to the Mayor's office, "We're getting along fine. Fine. Lots of fun being Mayor. Uh, have you been into the Mayor's office yet?"

"No. I just arrived, and then a man came in with a little complaint. The Mayor likes to handle such things himself, you know, so I asked him to come back on Monday."

I'll bet he likes to take care of them himself. Aloud, he said, "Well, why don't you go on home now. Nothing to do around here."

"I'll just go in and fill up your water pitcher for you."

"No need to do that!"

"Why, Mayor Fernald. You don't seem to *want* me to go in there."

"Well, uh, you see—well, we had lunch in there, and I'm afraid what's left of the pizza is sort of spread all over."

"I'll be glad to help clean it up."

"I'll clean it up," said the Pest quickly.

But the kids were too late. Miss Carner already had the door open, and was looking in amazement at the blanket of half-nibbled pizza spread all over the room.

"Well I must say," she said with a sniff of disapproval, "that you children have left the Mayor's office in quite a mess."

She crossed over toward the desk with Alvin at her heels. He knew exactly what she would see, and she saw it almost immediately because it rested on the only uncluttered part of the desk, as though framed in tomato sauce, cheese and sausage.

There, resting in the open spot, was the little leatherbound book from her desk. And just beside it was the sheet of paper with the plan of the new City Hall.

13

Locked In!

For what seemed a lifetime there was no movement, not a sound in the Mayor's office. The kids stood frozen by the door. Their eyes were on Miss Carner, who was staring at the little leatherbound book.

Suddenly she whirled. Her normally cold, blue eyes bore into Alvin's. It was the first time he'd seen any real expression in those eyes, and it frightened him. Alvin felt the Pest's hand creep into his.

When Miss Carner spoke it was in a low voice, but each word was spoken slowly and clearly. "What does this mean? What have you children been doing?"

No one replied.

"Answer me! These are the Mayor's private papers. What have you been doing with them?"

Surprisingly, it was the Pest who finally offered a reply. Alvin had always had the feeling that his little sister really was braver than he was, although he had never admitted it aloud. Now she was proving it.

The Pest's hand squeezed his. Then she said, "Miss Carner, if you're talking about that little book, I'm to blame for taking it from your desk. I was looking for some paper, and I found the book, and thought Alvin might like to see it, so I brought it into his office, and—"

"You are a sneak!" Miss Carner's words cut in sharply. She turned to Alvin. "And I suppose you found the book interesting?"

"Yes. Well. You see—" Alvin's parents had taught him never to lie, but in this case he thought a little fib might be forgiven. He thought desperately for a moment, then blurted, "You see, my little sister has been wanting a book to keep track of birthdays, and she told me this was the kind she wanted."

The Pest looked at him in amazement.

"And what about the piece of paper on that desk, in the middle of all that filth?" asked Miss Carner.

"Well, I guess—" stammered Alvin, "I guess— Well, I don't know how it got there."

"Do you know what the writing in that book, and on the piece of paper, mean?"

"No!" all three kids replied at the same moment. In their desire to be convincing they answered too promptly and too loudly.

Miss Carner turned her cold eyes on each of them in turn. Then she hissed, "You children are sneaks, all of you. I'm going now to find the Mayor. He'll know what to do about this. I may be gone for quite some time, as the golf tournament will be over by now, and I don't know exactly where to find him. Meanwhile you children will stay here." She moved past them, through the doorway.

"In fact," she said, just before she slammed the door, *"I'm going to lock you in."* Then, fainter, through the heavy panels of the door, they heard her say, "And it won't do you any good to try to get out. The Mayor and I have the only keys. I also am unplugging the phone. That will disconnect the phone in there, so don't try to call for help. While I'm gone, I suggest you start cleaning up that mess."

Alvin pressed his ear to the door. There was a rustling in the outer office, then silence.

"Hoooooorrrrrrg!" Speedy let out a sigh.

Alvin was still listening to make sure Miss Carner had departed. He crossed to the desk and lifted the telephone. The line was dead.

The kids were staring at each other when they heard the sound of running footsteps approaching the door. Was Miss Carner returning already? The door knob turned, but the door didn't open. Alvin crossed to the door and pressed his ear against one of the panels.

Suddenly there was a banging on the door, right against his ear. It was like an explosion inside his head, and he hopped around the room, holding his ear under the palm of his hand.

"Hey, Alvin!" came a faint voice through the

panels. "How c-c-c-come you've got the door locked? Lemme in! It's imp-p-p-portant!" No, that certainly wasn't Miss Carner!

Alvin jumped back to the door. "Listen, Worm," he said, the words tumbling out, "we're locked in. We can't get out. Miss Carner found us here, and she suspects we know about the Mayor being a crook. She's gone to find him."

"But it's important, Alvin! I've got to see you. I just g-g-got a reply from the FBI!"

Alvin thought for a moment. "Shove it under the door."

A moment later the corner of a sheet of yellow paper came sliding under the door. Alvin bent down and snatched it. When he straightened up, the other two kids were watching him eagerly. He read it aloud. The typewritten words seemed to leap out at him:

TO CHIEF OF POLICE RIVERTON. SUBJECT NAMED MELBOURNE MASSEY HAS LONG RECORD AS CONFIDENCE MAN. OTHER ALIASES JOHN THOMPSON, ARTHUR WHEATON, JAMES VERNER. USUAL METHOD OF OPERATION IS TO MOVE INTO COMMUNITY, GAIN CONFIDENCE OF CITIZENS, EVENTUALLY ESCAPE WITH PUBLIC FUNDS. PHYSICAL DESCRIPTION FOLLOWS: 6 FEET 2 INCHES TALL, WEIGHT 190, AGE 45, BLUE EYES, GRAYING HAIR, DISTINGUISHED APPEARANCE. USUALLY ACCOMPANIED BY ATTRACTIVE WOMAN APPROXIMATELY

35 TO 40 YEARS OLD. CITY OF SMITHVILLE FLOR-
IDA OFFERS $1000 REWARD FOR INFORMATION
LEADING TO APPREHENSION AND CONVICTION OF
THIS MAN. FBI.

14

Whummmmp!

At last they had the proof they needed!

"Worm!" shouted Alvin through the door. "Go tell Sergeant Mihaus to call my father on the radio and get him back here. Get him here immediately. Tell him it's *very* important, or Dad will think we're just clowning around. *Very important.*"

"G-g-gotcha. Are you going to have him break down the door?"

Alvin looked around the office. The cold pizza made it something of a mess, but that could be cleaned up. He had grown very fond of the office in the past few hours. *His* office, the office of Mayor Alvin Fernald. He looked at the sturdy oak door. It would be a shame to destroy it. No, there must be some other way out.

"Just get my dad back here immediately," he ordered. "Don't worry about the door. But before you leave, go over to Miss Carner's desk and plug the phone back into a socket you'll find somewhere down close to the floor. And after you send for my Dad, you might somehow get word to Shoie to ride back here on his bike as fast as he can."

Alvin listened to the footsteps scamper away, then went over and sat down behind the Mayor's desk. He lifted one edge of a pizza and reached underneath, so he could rub his finger along the smooth wood.

"I'm going to wait for Dad before I tell anyone about this," he said. "Nobody else is likely to believe our story. We have proof now, but the grownups may think we're just a bunch of kids trying to play a trick. I'm not sure even Dad will believe us at first." He looked up at the other two. "Now, how do we get out of here? I wouldn't want to smash down that beautiful door even if I thought we could."

There was a long silence.

As usual it was Speedy, the people-organizer, who came up with the germ of an idea. "Alvin," he asked suddenly, "who gets people out of buildings when they're in danger?"

"The Fire Department."

"Well, Peanuts Dunkle is your Fire Chief, and he's sitting over there in the firehouse right now."

Alvin thought for a moment, then leaped for the phone. He dialed the operator, and said, his voice ringing with authority, "Give me the Fire Department immediately!"

A moment later, "Hello is Peanuts Dunk—I mean is Fire Chief Dunkle there? . . . Hello, Peanuts? Mayor Fernald here. . . . Yeah, Alvin. Listen, Peanuts, this is very important. *I'm not kidding.* You understand? Okay. Get hold of the officer on duty, and tell him that there's a real emergency over at the City Hall. A *real* one. Lives may be in danger. . . . No kidding, Peanuts. Tell him to get the rescue truck over here right away. Pull it up on the south side of City Hall and get out that big round rescue net they use when they catch people jumping from burning buildings. . . .

"No, don't worry, Peanuts. I'll take the responsibility. Now, *do* it!" He slammed down the phone. He knew the firemen would have doubts about the call, but he also knew they wouldn't take a chance by refusing to answer *any* emergency call.

"Come on," he said, "let's get ready."

Carefully he folded the report from the FBI and the sheet of paper showing the foundation of the new City Hall. He slipped them into the little leather-bound book and stuffed it into his pocket. Speedy and the Pest followed him without a word as he walked over to the big window and opened it.

A moment later they heard the wail of a siren, then the rescue truck roared around the corner and stopped on the street below. Peanuts was riding up front beside the driver. His white helmet had settled all the way down over his ears, so he looked like he had no head.

The firemen jumped off the truck and snatched out the folded life net. It seemed to leap into existence in their trained hands—a big white circle.

They dashed over to the side of the building while the officer and Peanuts looked up toward the windows.

Alvin climbed onto the window ledge. It was only two stories high, but from here the life net seemed very small and very far away. His knees began to tremble, and his hands, which were clamped tightly to the window behind him, were growing slippery.

Alvin Fernald was scared. He took a deep breath, closed his eyes, and let go of the window. He jumped.

There was a roaring in his ears, which he suddenly recognized as his own voice. Just for a split second he opened his eyes and saw the tip of his own shoe floating against the sky. Then he landed.

Whummmmmmp.

"Ooooooooooofff!"

He looked over at Speedy, who had landed beside him.

At the same moment both boys realized what might happen next, and scrambled for the edge of the net. Alvin glanced up and saw his sister sailing through the air, skirt flying around her little legs.

Whummmmmmp.

"Gee, Alvin," she said from the middle of the net, grinning across at him, "that was the most fun I've ever had in my life! Can we do it again, Alvin? Can we?"

"Young man, I hope you have an explanation for

this." It was the voice of the officer in charge of the firemen.

Before Alvin could reply there was the wail of a siren, and a police car screeched to a stop just behind the rescue truck. Dad leaped out and ran toward them.

"Alvin, I hope you have an explanation for this!"

Alvin, on his hands and knees atop the fire net, stared at the firemen, then at Dad. He looked beyond them, still dazed, and saw Shoie riding up on his bike. Alvin shook his head from side to side, trying to clear it.

Then Mayor Fernald took over once more. "Shoie," he called, "get all the kids together on the playground at Roosevelt School."

"You're not going anywhere," said his father. "You're going to explain what's happening here."

"Yeah," said Alvin. "That's what I want to do. Can we go inside, Dad?"

15

Emergency Plan

Ten minutes later the police department went quietly but efficiently into action.

It hadn't taken Alvin nearly as long as he'd thought it would to convince Dad that Mayor Massey was, indeed, a criminal, and had been stealing from the city. At first Dad had seemed a bit skeptical when Alvin described his suspicions of the Mayor, with many interruptions from Speedy and the Pest, and a few stammered ones from Worm. Then Alvin had produced the leatherbound book, and the evidence of cheating in construction of the new City Hall. And finally, when he'd brought out the message from the FBI, Dad had instantly accepted everything they'd said.

He had taken a moment to look levelly across his desk at the four kids. Then he'd turned his attention to Alvin alone. "Son, I won't deny that you've done the city some good today. And, in some ways, I'm very proud of you. But you could have trusted me with this information sooner than you did. Because you *didn't* trust me to believe you, two criminals may escape. You've given them a head start." He had paused, and Alvin thought there was the faintest suggestion of a smile on his face. "And that rescue act with the fire net was completely unnecessary."

Now, after that mild lecture, the four kids were alone in Dad's office. Through the open door they could hear Dad and Sergeant Milhaus arranging the search for Mayor Massey and Miss Carner, then setting up police roadblocks on all the highways in case the two criminals tried to escape.

Alvin should have felt excited, even proud, but for some reason he didn't. He was just plain tired. From his chair behind Dad's desk he watched as Speedy walked over and closed the door, shutting out the quiet but urgent voices of the police officers.

"Well, I guess we did it," said Alvin.

"Not quite," said Speedy.

"What do you mean?"

"Well, the job won't be finished until Mayor Massey and Miss Carney are arrested."

"Dad will take care of that."

"I'm not so sure, Alvin."

Alvin bristled. Dad knew his job better than any police officer in Riverton. "What do you mean?"

"Well, I've been thinking. Come on into that teletype room with me."

Alvin didn't know what was up, but got wearily

to his feet and followed the others into the little room with the clacking typewriter.

Speedy shut the door behind them. He looked up at one wall of the room. "What do you see there?" he asked.

The other kids followed his gaze. A map of Riverton had been taped to the wall. Heavy red lines had been drawn across the highways around the edges of the city.

It was Police Chief Worm Wormley who answered Speedy's question. "It's a p-p-plan for setting up roadblocks when they're needed."

"Right." Speedy's eyelids were beginning to close, which was a sure sign that he was thinking deeply. "Alvin, do you know whether Mayor Massey spent any time in this room?"

Alvin suddenly was alert. "Yes. He did. Dad said he often dropped into police headquarters." He thought for a moment. "Looking back, I suppose he wanted to keep track of what the police were doing because he was a criminal."

"And being a criminal, what would he be most likely to check carefully, here in police headquarters?"

Instantly Alvin knew what Speedy was driving at. "Why, he'd want to plan an escape route if anything ever happened. So that map on the wall would be the most important thing of all to him."

Speedy spoke very softly. "I'll bet he has the map memorized. I'll bet he sees those red lines in his sleep."

Riverton

bill sokol

"I'll see those red lines, too," said Worm. "At least t-t-tonight. As Police Chief, I spent most of my time looking at the map. You see," he said a bit sheepishly, "there wasn't really much for me to do."

"And I'll bet Mayor Massey already has an escape route worked out that avoids all those road-blocks," said Speedy.

"Hey," said Worm brightly. "So do I! With nothing else to do, I figured just how I'd get out of t-t-town if I ever had to." He paused. "Of course, I don't figure I'll ever have to."

Alvin suddenly was excited. "Quick, Worm. We don't have time to study that map, but you've already done it. If *you* were a criminal, and wanted to escape by car, how would you get out of town?"

"Well, all the main highways and even the side roads are covered. It took quite a while to figure it out. Kind of like a p-p-puzzle, you know. Anyway, if you go out Third Street you come to a narrow dirt road that ends up at the city dump. At least most people think it ends there. Here, I'll show you on the map. But if you go around the edge of the dump to the other side, the road continues on, right here. See the dotted line? Anyway, the road goes on for about eight miles to a c-c-county road, which eventually joins up with Highway eighty-three. And there's no red line marked anywhere along the way."

Alvin gave a low whistle. Suddenly he wasn't tired any longer. "Worm, I'll bet you're right. I know that area pretty well. We've gone out there a lot to pick over the junk, and to fish in the creek that runs along just this side of the dump."

He walked over and flung open the door. "Dad!" he called.

Sergeant Fernald, obviously impatient because of the interruption, came into the room.

Quickly the kids explained their theory.

"I don't know," Sergeant Fernald said doubtfully, after thinking it over. "It's pretty farfetched. I really question whether Massey has thought that far ahead." Alvin noticed that Dad had dropped the title "Mayor" from the man's name.

"Anyway," Dad continued, "we have every available man assigned to the highway roadblocks. I think we'll nab him at one of them, if we don't locate him around town first. There's just no squad car left—or men, for that matter—to put out on that dirt road. We've sent out a statewide alert, and we'll just have to take the chance that if we should miss him, he'll be caught further down the line." He crossed toward the door.

The Magnificent Brain leaped into action. "Okay, Dad. Whatever you say. But look. Do you have a patrol car going over toward Roosevelt School?"

"In about two minutes we'll have one leaving that will go within a block of the school."

"Could we ride along? The kids are all waiting for me over there, see, to inspect some stuff they've been doing around town—"

"Yes, I've heard about those playgrounds," Dad

interrupted with a smile. "Okay. I'll have the squad drop you at school. That's the least we can do for Mayor Fernald. Come along."

Five minutes later the squad car, siren wailing, pulled up beside the school. All the kids were there, some of them playing baseball, but they all came running when they heard the siren. A mighty cheer shook the schoolgrounds when Alvin stepped out, followed by the others.

"Mayor Fernald," said a loud voice, "I am the chairman in charge of the Welcoming Committee."

Alvin groaned. It was Theresa Undermine, starting one of her long speeches.

"We of Miss Pinkney's class of the fifth grade of Roosevelt School feel honored that—" She stopped because her voice was drowned by the wail of the siren as the police car pulled away toward its assigned roadblock.

"We of Miss Pinkney's class—"

"Theresa, doggone it, we don't have time for a speech." When she looked hurt, he added, "You can make it later. I promise. Now help me get all the kids over to the steps."

When they were all assembled, amid a good many hoots and hollers, Alvin climbed up on the top step.

"My good friends and fellow citizens of Riverton," he began, almost automatically. Then he stopped and said, "Let's forget all that junk. Look, kids. Maybe—just maybe—we can help capture two criminals."

Quickly he told the kids everything they'd learned about Mayor Massey. The playground became absolutely quiet except for his voice. As he spoke, the thought flashed through his mind that this was one difference between kids and adults; kids automatically believed another kid—at least when they *knew* he was serious—but you had to *prove* things to adults.

"Anyway," he said in conclusion, "we figure Mayor Massey is still in town. The police haven't located him yet, and besides, Miss Carner said it might take *her* a while to find him. Then she and the Mayor will have to go get the money they've taken, wherever they've hidden it, before they head out of town. We're almost sure what route they'll take, and there's no one guarding it. Now can we —Miss Pinkney's class—do something to stop them?"

A roar went up from the kids. Shoelace McCafferty shouted that he'd get his slingshot; Luella Shaner, swept away by her enthusiasm, offered to lie down in front of the Mayor's car; and Willy Davis offered to run home and get the ultimate weapon, his little brother Evil Eye.

"Wait!" shouted Alvin above the uproar. "Wait! We don't have much time. I want to talk to the following guys on the pitcher's mound of the baseball field: Shoie, Speedy, Worm and Spider. We have to do some planning. Meanwhile I want the rest of you—as Mayor I *order* the rest of you—to run home as fast as you can, get your bikes, and come back here."

The kids scattered as though a bomb had gone off in their midst. Alvin trotted over to the pitcher's mound with the four boys—and the uninvited Pest—at his heels.

Mayor Fernald was at a loss for words. He didn't have the remotest plan for stopping Mayor Massey. He took a deep breath, held it a moment, then said, "Anybody got any good ideas?"

Thirty seconds of silence passed. Then the ideas came gushing out.

Shoie wanted to spread nails all over the road to puncture the Mayor's tires; Alvin ruled that out because they'd also damage other people's tires. Worm suggested they flood the dirt road with water, making it such a gooey mess that the Mayor's car would get stuck; Alvin reminded him that they didn't have any place to connect a hose. The Pest wanted to collect all the flypaper in town and somehow (she never quite figured it out) stick the Mayor's car to the road. Alvin didn't even argue with her.

But soon the kids started coming up with ideas that sounded wild, yet possible. And after talking them over, they settled on a plan.

Alvin ticked off the supplies they'd need: "A couple of gunnysacks?"

"I'll get them right now, and the rope, too," said Shoie. He ran for his bike.

"A shovel?"

"We've g-g-got one in the garage. My house is right on the way, and we'll pick it up as we ride past."

The Pest suddenly had a brilliant idea. "Alvin, why don't I run home and bring back those two walkie-talkies you got for Christmas?"

"Good idea," said Alvin, turning to his sister. "They might come in handy for communications."

She flitted away, her golden hair streaming out behind.

Five minutes later most of the kids in the class were back with their bikes.

"Okay," said Alvin crisply to Speedy and Worm, before they joined the others. "It's a good plan. Should work. But remember, we don't want to take a chance on any of the other kids getting hurt. Mayor Massey is a criminal, and may be dangerous. I think we can stop him ourselves, just Shoie and Speedy and me. But in an emergency we'll have to rely on the other kids. In that case, Worm, you'll be in charge because you're Chief of Police. And the main thing is, don't let any of the kids take any chances. We don't want anyone hurt. Okay, guys. Let's get going!"

16

Preparations for an Ambush

The kids, all thirty of them, came riding over the top of the hill just outside of town, bicycle spokes flashing in the late afternoon sunlight.

It was a strange procession. In the lead was Shoie with Alvin riding on the bar of his bike, trying to hang on with one hand while he held a long shovel in the other.

Just behind was Spider Funsterman, the Pest perched on his handlebar. She was perfectly balanced, scarcely bothering to hang on at all. With one hand she held a walkie-talkie to her ear, and she was listening to the crackle-pop, and occasionally the faint voice, that squawked from the earphone.

Behind Spider came Worm, with the other kids strung out behind on bikes of all shapes, sizes and descriptions.

And bringing up the rear was Speedy Glomitz, riding on the bar of Peanuts Dunkle's bike, desperately trying to operate the other walkie-talkie. Alvin had posted him back there to keep his eye on the rear, in case the Mayor's car came sooner than expected.

At the top of the hill, Alvin had Shoie stop the procession so they could look over the lay of the land. The rutted dirt road plunged down into a little valley. There it crossed a creek that Alvin knew very well, for in its shallows swam chubs and other small fish and along its banks a sharp-eyed kid could find green frogs and small snapping turtles. On the other side of the creek the road lifted again, passing under some huge and leafy oaks, and disappeared over the top of the next hill. Alvin knew that just beyond, but out of sight, was the old city dump, littered with trash, bottles, tires, tin cans, old cars, smashed furniture and almost everything else imaginable.

Quickly he looked over the kids, who by now had gathered around. "I need someone for a very important job." His eyes swept over Theresa Undermine, then came back to her again. She had a defiant look on her face. She probably was feeling that way because she'd lost the election, and because he hadn't even given her time to make her welcoming speech back on the school playground.

"Theresa!" he barked. "I'm going to give you the most important job of all. I want you to hide yourself and your bike over in those bushes. Speedy, give her your walkie-talkie and show her how to use it." Quickly Speedy did so. "Now, Theresa, you're our lookout. That's very important. If you see a car coming, it probably will be the Mayor. You push the button on that radio transmitter and let us know. Okay?"

Theresa nodded, eyes now flashing, obviously proud of her assignment.

"The rest of you kids follow Worm over the next hill, to the city dump. I don't want any of you to be seen from here. Worm will tell you what to do and when to do it. Follow his orders *exactly;* don't forget, he's still Chief of Police around here. Okay, let's go."

Alvin and Shoie shoved off and coasted down the hill, the other kids following. At the bottom, where the creek rippled under the old concrete bridge, Alvin and Shoie stopped and waited. As the other kids rode past, Speedy slipped off Peanuts' bike. The Pest, too—without permission—joined the little group. The rest of the kids pedaled on up the hill and disappeared over the crest.

"Pest, you keep listening for Theresa on the walkie-talkie. The rest of us know what to do. Let's do it!"

Shoie shoved his bike off the road and hid it in some tall weeds down by the creek. Speedy and Shoie joined him there, carrying the shovel, gunny-sacks and rope. Hurriedly they found a particularly swampy little area covered with black mud and little rivulets of water.

"Well, here goes," said Alvin. He took a deep breath and stepped into the mud. Promptly his good

Sunday shoes disappeared in the muck. A moment later he was standing knee-deep in the gooey stuff. "Perfect!" he said, a happy smile on his face.

Speedy and Shoie slurped in after him. Alvin held the gunnysacks open while the other two boys filled them with mud.

"I'm supposed to be working behind the scenes," said Speedy, "figuring out how to get other people to do the work. Remember?" But there was a grin on his face.

The job finished, the boys slooped and sloshed their way out of the little swamp, carrying the two heavy bags. They hid the shovel with Shoe's bike, and managed to wrestle the bags up onto the road.

Shoie was in the middle as they headed on up the hill because he was the biggest and strongest, holding a corner of a sack in each hand. The other two boys staggered along beside him, helping with the load.

The Pest brought up the rear, still in her pretty yellow dress, the rope slung across her shoulder and the walkie-talkie constantly pressed to her ear.

"I didn't know mud was so heavy," gasped Alvin. He had his eyes on two huge oak trees, one on each side of the rutted road, about halfway up the hill. Their foliage joined in a thick clump above the roadway. Beneath the trees he stopped.

"Quick," he said to the Pest, "give Shoie the rope." He knew they had to hurry. Mayor Massey, if he came this way at all, would appear at any moment.

Shoie tied the rope to the top of one sack while Speedy boosted Alvin up into the lower branches of one of the trees. Alvin climbed out along a huge branch until he was directly above the road. Without a word spoken, the rope whistled up. He reached out to catch it, almost lost his balance, and felt the rope smack into his hand. Quickly he dropped it on the other side of the branch.

Below, Speedy and Shoie grabbed the loose end and pulled. Majestically the bag of mud rose into the air, dripping a steady brown stream. When the sack hit the bottom of the limb, Alvin managed to reach down, clasp it to his chest, and heave it up into the tree. It felt cold and slimy even through his good shirt. He and the mudbag almost went right on over the other side of the limb, but he finally managed to balance it in the tree.

By the time Alvin had the rope untied, Speedy had climbed out along the limb beside him.

The process was repeated with the other bag, except that this time the Pest had to help Shoie by lending her slight weight to the rope. She was standing almost directly under the bag as it rose slowly into the air, and the muddy water streamed down across her blond curls and onto her good dress.

The sight made Alvin shudder. Mom would be horrified. But far from bothering the Pest, she seemed to *like* it. She even stuck the tip of her tongue out of the corner of her mouth. Quickly she drew it back in, then made a face. "It *looks*

115

like chocolate, but it sure doesn't *taste* like chocolate," she said.

Moments later, Alvin and Speedy had their legs locked around the big limb, two bags of mud balanced between them. The rope swished down.

Peering down through the leaves, Alvin saw Shoie tie one end of the rope to one of the trees, then dash across the road, pull the rope taut, and tie the other end to the other tree.

As a finishing touch the Pest, without even being told, placed the walkie-talkie on the ground, took off her once-beautiful hair ribbon—now a dirty yellow—and tied it to the rope in the middle of the road.

"Toss up the walkie-talkie," ordered Alvin.

Shoie picked it up and collapsed the antenna. Pivoting on one foot, he made a perfect hook shot into the tree. It was the same shot that had won many a basketball game for Roosevelt School. Alvin caught the radio as it sailed right through the leaves and into his lap.

"Hide!" he said urgently. "If Mayor Massey is coming at all, he'll come soon. *And don't take any chances!*"

Shoie and the Pest disappeared behind one of the big oak trees.

17

Conversation on a Tree Limb

"Do you suppose he'll come, Alvin?"

"I dunno, Speedy." Long pause. Then, "If he doesn't, we're going to look pretty silly."

"Yeah, I've been thinking about that, too. We got all those kids pretty excited, and then brought them out here. They're going to think we're mighty stupid if nothing happens. And it's all my fault, Alvin. I was the one who figured Mayor Massey might try to escape past the roadblocks."

"That's okay. I'll take the responsibility. After all, I'm the Mayor—at least for today."

Pause.

"Alvin, I've done some thinking. I used to think I was pretty smart, the way I could kind of push people around without them even knowing it. I thought it was fun, just to get other kids to do what I wanted."

"Yeah. You're pretty good at that. I've felt you push me around a good many times."

"But I learned something today. I found out I was scared—just plain scared. Maybe you didn't know it, Alvin, but I was even scared about putting up that stop sign. I didn't want anybody to blame me for breaking the law, or doing something wrong. And I'd have hid under the bed before I'd have sent that message to the FBI. But you didn't even think twice about it." Pause. "I guess I'm just a coward."

"Nope. You stuck by me all the time, Speedy. I'll admit it made me mad when you put your feet on my desk. But that kind of stuff isn't really important. What is important is that I'd still be sitting like a stuffed shirt in the Mayor's chair if you hadn't made me do things. It was your idea to put up the stop sign, and build the playgrounds, and chase out the peddlers, and start a new bus route for old Mrs. Toomey." Sudden pause. "Hey! Come to think of it, we didn't do anything about that bus route, did we?"

"I guess we just didn't have time, Mr. Mayor."

"Well, we did accomplish quite a bit—together—didn't we?"

"Maybe that's the secret."

"What's the secret?"

"Doing things together."

Crackle and pop from the walkie-talkie. Alvin glued it to his ear and heard a faint, excited voice. "Alvin! Your primary lookout, stationed on top of Hill X, keen of eyesight and always alert, wishes to report. Are you there?"

"Doggone it, Theresa, this is no time for a speech! Is a car coming?"

"Oh, yes, Alvin! It's not a long black car like the Mayor usually drives. It's sort of a chartreuse color, maybe a little bit more on the yellow side, and has cute little chromium stripes along the side. It's coming pretty slow because of the bumps in the road, but I can see that there are two people in it. A man and a woman. They're closer now. She's wearing a kind of a feathery hat that doesn't really go very well with what I can see of her dress. It's kind of a businessy dress, if you know what I mean, and the hat seems kind, of well, kind of formal to be worn with it. Anyway, maybe she—oh, Alvin, it *is* the Mayor! I can see him now. What'll I do, Alvin, what'll I do?" Sudden silence.

"Theresa, you did a great job. Now, as soon as the Mayor drives past, run down into the valley through the weeds, so you won't be seen, and then on up to the old city dump. Get there just as fast as you can because the kids there may need the walkie-talkie. Got it?"

"Yes, Alvin. Oh, Alvin, this is so exciting!"

Alvin took a deep breath. Then he grinned uncertainly at his buddy and said softly, "He's coming. Get ready!"

18

Captured!

"Pssssst! He's coming!" Alvin called softly down to Shoie and the Pest.

Through a hole in the leaves he could see the hem of his sister's flared skirt, and the tip of Shoie's elbow. They were hiding behind the big oak on the left side of the road.

Alvin wedged the walkie-talkie between two branches to free both hands. Then he cautiously pushed aside some leaves to get a better view. His heart was thumping wildly, and there seemed to be a big glop in his throat that kept him from breathing easily. It was almost like the time he'd had the flu, and his mother had put a vaporizer in the bedroom with him.

He got his first view of the car as it nosed over the top of the hill where Theresa had been stationed. It was indeed moving very slowly, weaving a bit, as the driver tried to avoid the bigger ruts in the road.

Once, to get past a particularly big hole, the Mayor stopped the car, backed up, and eased forward all the way over to the side of the road, the tires riding along the edge of the ditch.

But slowly and surely the car moved down the hill, and the closer it approached the less sure Alvin was that his two-part plan would work. If the first scheme failed, the second might succeed. Or so they'd thought. But now both schemes seemed childish, like daydreams of how you'd catch a burglar in your house at night. So many things could go wrong.

And what if one of the kids got hurt? He'd really be to blame. He was sorry, now, that he hadn't left the whole thing in Dad's hands. Even if the Mayor escaped (and it now was obvious that he'd bypassed the police roadblocks), he'd probably be caught someday. Maybe it would be better to call the whole thing off.

No! The Mayor had stolen the city's money, and had to be captured. And the only thing between him and his safe escape was Miss Pinkney's class, Room 3B, Roosevelt School—sixteen boys and fourteen girls. Plus two slimy sacks of mud.

The car had reached the bottom of the hill, and crawled slowly across the little bridge. Now it was turning upward again, less than a block away.

Alvin, his hand holding aside a few of the leaves just in front of his face, suddenly felt a prickly sensation on his wrist. He shifted his gaze slightly and saw a tiny spider crawl upward until it was on the back of his hand. There it stopped, no more than three inches from his eye.

When Alvin forced himself to look away from the spider, he saw that the car had stopped just a little distance away. He could guess what had happened. The Mayor was close enough now that he could see the rope stretched across the road between the two trees.

A head popped out of the car window. No doubt about it, it was Mayor Massey. The man took a long look up the road past the trees, as though he suspected that something was wrong. Then his head disappeared, and the car once more moved slowly up the hill.

Alvin gave a long sigh, and let loose of the branches in case his face should be seen. To avoid thinking about the Mayor, he held his hand up in front of his face and watched the spider again. By now it had crawled across his hand until it was at the base of his thumb, and seemed hesitant about what route to take from there.

It was at that moment, still looking down at the spider on his thumb, that Alvin saw the hood of the car slide into view just below his feet. It crept slowly forward, not more than six feet below, until the windshield was directly beneath the big limb. He could even see the Mayor's knees through the slanted windshield, one easing forward to put on the brake.

This was it!

Alvin took a deep breath and seemed to gag. But at the same moment, with a mighty heave, he toppled over his bag, keeping a tight hold on the bottom of it.

Alvin had expected—and planned—that the mud would pour out in a stream to cover the windshield. Instead it dropped out in one huge mudball, plummeting downward intact, like a gigantic meteorite from the sky.

Splat!

The mudball hit the windshield almost exactly in the center, and splayed outward in every direction, instantly and completely covering the glass.

A direct hit!

In his excitement, Alvin could only guess the sensations of the man and woman inside the car. One instant they were looking through the windshield at the rope stretched across the road. A split second later the view was simply wiped off the face of the earth, as though some gigantic hand had reached down and covered the glass. As far as moving forward, they were blind.

The kids had planned to stop the car only for a few moments—just time enough for Shoie to do his job. Alvin had figured that two mudballs would be required, one for each side of the windshield. Now Alvin's ball had hit dead center, wiping out the entire windshield instantly.

Still, he thought, it wouldn't hurt to drop the other mudball. In fact, Speedy should have dropped it by now. He glanced across and saw Speedy struggling. The bag was sagging between two branches, and Speedy was having difficulty dumping it. Alvin reached out one hand to help, grabbed the bag, and gave a tremendous shove.

The sudden movement threw Speedy off balance, and he reached outward for a branch. His fingers barely touched it, and then he went twisting out of the tree.

Alvin watched in horror as Speedy vanished. At the same instant he heard the slam of a car door, and glancing downward, saw the Mayor standing beside the car, peering up into the tree.

Splat!

The second mudball hit the Mayor full in the face, plastering his glasses right against his eyelids and encasing his entire head in a two-inch layer of mud.

"Oooof!" The Mayor, staggered by the blow, stumbled away from the car.

Thunnkk!

Speedy had done a somersault in midair, and came crashing down on the hood of the car.

Sssssssssssssssst! Shoie was already at work letting air out of one of the rear tires.

But Alvin, sitting on the tree limb, was horrified at what happened next.

The Mayor blindly staggered toward the oak tree, brushing his sleeve across his eyes. His glasses fell to the ground, but it seemed to make no difference. He was simply trying to *see* again, and when he could see, at least dimly, the first thing he saw was the Pest poking her head around the trunk of the tree.

The Mayor's hand reached out, fast as a snake, and grabbed her arm. He jerked her to him, then whirled around toward the car. Speedy was sitting on the hood, dazed, and Shoie was trying to let the air out of the tire with shaking fingers.

"Stop!" said the Mayor. His voice was low and venomous. "Get away from that car!"

Both Speedy and Shoie looked up. Still dazed, Speedy rolled off the hood and stood there beside the car.

Psssssssssssssst! Shoie, bravest of the brave, continued to let out the air.

"Stop, or this girl will be hurt."

Instantly the sound of escaping air ceased. Alvin sighed in relief. Good old Shoie!

"I should break you kids into pieces," said the Mayor in a low, flat voice. "But I haven't time. Now untie that rope and get away from that car! I'm taking this girl with us, just to make sure you don't try anything else."

Still wiping the mud off his head with one hand while he held the Pest with the other, Mayor Massey walked around the car and opened the door. Miss Carner was sitting inside, a bewildered expression on her face, a metal box beside her on the seat.

The Mayor thrust the Pest inside. "Hold her," he said.

Apparently the Mayor was still unaware of Alvin's existence directly overhead. Alvin wished he had another mudball. He watched while Shoie untied the rope and let it drop to the ground across the road.

Meanwhile the Mayor was wiping the windshield with his sleeve. Satisfied at last that he could peer through a small circle in the murky glass, he climbed into the car beside Miss Carner and the Pest.

"Remember," he called through the window, "just one wrong move and this girl will suffer."

The car edged forward. The left rear tire was low but not flat. The boys had hoped to delay the Mayor just long enough to let the air out of two of the tires, so the car couldn't move, but they had failed.

Now the car not only could move, but the Pest was inside.

Perched in the tree, Alvin felt dizzy, almost sick to his stomach. Doggone it, he *had* to do something, and right now.

There was still one chance. He reached out for the walkie-talkie, wedged between the limbs, but in his confused state he misjudged the distance. The back of his hand hit the radio, and he watched horrified as it began to slip out of the tree. At the last moment, just as it fell, he reached out and scooped it up.

"Hello, Theresa! *Tell Worm to give the signal to the kids right now! And tell them to be careful. Mayor Massey has my little sister in that car!*"

With the radio in one hand, he grabbed a tree branch in the other and swung down until he was dangling over the road. He let go, bent his knees to cushion his fall, and found himself face down in the dirt. When he scrambled to his feet he was standing in the road, Shoie on one side and Speedy on the other.

The boys didn't even glance at each other, nor was a single word spoken. Their eyes were fixed, not on the car as it climbed slowly upward, but on the top of the hill.

It seemed that hours passed before the first head popped into view, outlined against the sky immediately followed by others. Suddenly there they all were, in full glory, the kids of Room 3B, Roosevelt School. They were lined up as though in formation, almost like an Indian movie. But there were no bows or rifles in their hands.

Instead, each kid's hand rested on an old tire from the city dump.

Even at this distance Alvin could see that it was Worm who fired the first volley. He brushed the top of his tire with his hand to get it rolling, took three or four quick steps, then gave it a final push on its way.

The tire started slowly at first. In fact, to Alvin it didn't seem to be moving at all. Then it wobbled a bit, righted itself, and picked up speed as it moved down the steep hill.

Worm's aim had been good. The tire came

straight down the road, bouncing now and then as it hit a rut, rolling faster and faster.

As it approached the car, the tire seemed to lean just a bit to the left, and the car almost instantly pulled to the right. The tire whipped past at tremendous speed.

But the car, now on the right side of the road, was too late to veer away from the second tire, which was already on the road. In fact, *four* tires were now rolling down the hill at the same time. The first one headed straight for the mayor's car, and there was no possible way he could avoid it. Then, at the last moment, the tire hit a deep rut running across the road, and bounded high into the air. It cleared the roof of the car by a whisper, and went bounding off into the ditch.

Alvin had been paralyzed at the sight of the hurtling tires, but now the excited cheers from the top of the hill broke through into the Magnificent Brain. He answered with a wild cry of his own. Suddenly he was running up the hill, Speedy and Shoie at his heels.

By now there was a fairly steady parade of tires rolling down the hill. Most quickly veered off into the ditches (the aim of the girls wasn't too good), but a few chased each other down the road. As each one approached, the car twisted this way or that as the Mayor made a desperate effort to dodge out of its way.

He must know, thought Alvin, *that his only chance of escape is to reach the top of the hill.*

It was Peanuts and Alicia, working together, who finally stopped the car.

Alvin was watching the top of the hill as he ran, and he saw the two kids struggle into view with, incredibly, a tractor tire much taller than they were. Balancing it in position, Alicia suddenly let go, and Peanuts gave it such a mighty shove that he fell flat on his face. The other kids, awestruck by the sight of the tremendous missile, stopped to watch.

The tire wobbled from side to side at first, as though it would fall, but finally straightened out as it picked up speed. Then it was moving majestically down the road, so huge and heavy that the ruts didn't have the slightest effect on it.

Worm started hollering first, then the other kids took up the cry. Alvin found himself answering back. Somehow it was like an exciting ballgame, and this was the play that would decide the championship. There was a swelling roar from the stands as victory—or defeat—hung in the balance.

The Mayor could not have helped but hear the roar of the stands and see the invincible, unstoppable march of destiny toward him. The car stopped for a moment as the towering tire hurtled toward it. Then, in a final act of desperation, the Mayor whipped the car over to the right of the road. There it skidded to a stop, two wheels in the ditch.

As the big tire sailed past, just inches from the door, the Mayor tried to put the car into motion again, but the rear wheels spun uselessly, grinding deeper into the ditch.

The door opened and the Mayor leaped out. He took one look around, then started running up the road toward the kids.

At that moment Worm Wormley, Chief of Police (for one day) of Riverton, Indiana, let fly the last bullet in his gun, the last tire in the city dump.

It was just an ordinary old tire, worn until there was no tread left, aged by sun and wind, but it seemed to have a mind of its own.

Alvin was close behind the Mayor by now, and saw the man slow down when the tire lunged toward him. As the Mayor jumped to the right, it promptly veered to the right. When he desperately leaped to the left, the tire turned with him. It moved as though it had eyes. And each instant that passed brought the tire that much closer, and moving that much faster.

Suddenly fearful, the man stopped, then backed up, still facing his rolling doom. At the last moment, with the tire only a few feet away, he lunged desperately through the air toward the ditch.

His feet were off the ground when the tire struck the very tip of one of his shoes. The blow twisted him in a circle in midair, and he seemed to hover there like a helicopter for a long moment before he plummeted to the ground.

He struck with a plop and lay still.

Alvin, exhausted from the long run up the hill, suddenly saw the Pest race past him like the wind. In the commotion, she must have escaped from

Miss Carner. Horrified, he watched her run straight over to the motionless figure of Mayor Massey.

"Stay away!" he shouted. "Stay away! He may still be dangerous!"

She was bending over the man's feet as Alvin skidded to a stop beside her. "His shoe!" she said urgently without even looking up. "Get his other shoe!"

"Why?"

"You'll see." She had untied one shoe and now jerked it off. Alvin promptly pulled off the other shoe, feeling the man's leg come to life as he did so.

The two kids backed away as the man slowly got to his hands and knees, shook his head back and forth to clear it, then climbed to his feet. He stood there, swaying slightly, but gazing at them with cold eyes.

"You kids are responsible for this." He spat out the words and started moving toward them.

"This way, Alvin," said the Pest in her high, sweet voice, as though they were in the back yard playing hide and seek. Still clutching the shoe, she scampered across the ditch to the weeds beyond.

Alvin followed—and so did the man.

Mayor Massey, flinching with every step, made it up the far side of the ditch to the edge of the weeds. Suddenly he jumped backward as though he'd touched an electric fence. He moved to one side, took two steps forward, and fell back again.

"What—" began Alvin, thoroughly mystified.

"Thistles and cockleburs," said his little sister sweetly. "Come on, Alvin. Let's play catch with his shoes while he watches."

The kids had assembled in the weedfield near the road. Twice Miss Carner had started to get out of the car, then thought better of it when Shoie and half a dozen of the other bigger boys started toward her.

Alvin was trying to decide what to do next when he heard the siren. He looked across the little valley and saw the police car, trailing a plume of dust, roll down the rutted road and across the little bridge.

The car climbed the hill and slammed to a stop. Dad and Sergeant Milhaus jumped out, revolvers drawn.

"Are you kids all right?" Dad called anxiously.

"Sure, Dad, we're just fine. Except, well, except I got my good clothes kind of dirty. How did you know we were out here?"

"I got your radio message."

Alvin's mind was a blank. "What radio message?"

"Those walkie-talkies of yours happen to be on the same wavelength as the squad car radios." His eyes twinkled. "That's against the law, you know. You'll have to retune them to another frequency. Anyway, we heard you talking to Theresa—I think that was her name—and you told her that Massey had your little sister in the car. I had a good idea where you were, so we came out here immediately."

"We sure are glad to see you, Dad. We didn't know what to do with them next."

Sergeant Fernald looked at the car in the ditch, Miss Carner still in the front seat. Her face was as expressionless as ever.

He shifted his gaze to the man seated in the roadway, his face in his hands. At that moment the man looked up. His face was covered with mud, and his eyes were two white blobs. The mud had splattered down across his expensive blue suit, giving it a horrible two-tone effect. There were no shoes on his feet, and his socks were in ribbons. One big toe, where it stuck through a hole, was bleeding.

But the most striking part of the man, though it could hardly be seen through the mud, was the expression of utter defeat on his face. Mayor Massey—*former* Mayor Massey—had given up.

"It doesn't look like you kids need much help to handle these two," said Dad.

19

A Shortage in the City Treasury

It was almost eight o'clock in the evening by the time Alvin and the Pest arrived at Wormley's Ice Cream Shoppe.

They'd been mighty busy meanwhile, but a good kind of busy.

Out on the dusty road, Dad had handcuffed Massey and Miss Carner together, and put them in the patrol car. He'd found the metal box on the front seat of the Mayor's car. Alvin and the other kids watched as he opened it. It was filled with $100 bills.

"It probably belongs to the city," Dad said quietly. "That will be up to the court to determine. But if it *is* money stolen from the city, or money taken illegally by Massey while he occupied the Mayor's office, then it will be returned—thanks to you kids."

Alvin made a date to meet the rest of the kids at 7:30 that night for ice cream sundaes, as he had promised. Then he and the Pest rode back to town in the patrol car.

It was an eerie feeling, sitting there in the front seat with Dad, while Massey and Miss Carner rode in the back seat under the watchful eye of Sergeant Milhaus. Not a word was said. Once Alvin glanced back over his shoulder. Massey was sitting there with his chin on his chest, completely beaten, paying no attention to what was happening, but Miss Carner glared at Alvin with a look of pure hatred.

At the station, Dad wrote out some papers concerning the two criminals, and led them away to jail cells. He then obtained permission from the Chief of Police to drive "Mayor Fernald and his private secretary" home.

Alvin walked right through the door, went upstairs, and took a long bath. It was such an unusual thing for him to do that his mother immediately began to fret.

"Something's wrong with Alvin," he heard her say to Dad through the door. "I *know* something's wrong with that boy."

Then, at dinner, he was so tired from all the excitement of the day that he wasn't hungry. Besides, he'd been burping pizza all afternoon. After only a few bites of pot roast he asked to be excused.

"I knew you were sick," said Mom. "You'd better go to bed this minute."

"Can't," said Alvin, putting on his jacket. "I'm still Mayor, and I still have one thing left to do. But I'll be home early, Mom. Don't worry."

The door slammed behind him. It slammed again a moment later as the Pest slipped out, uninvited, and chased him down the street.

Now, as they approached Wormley's Ice Cream Shoppe, Alvin could see the other kids inside. Speedy and Shoie were waiting on the outside step, and when they saw Alvin coming they opened the door a crack and shouted something inside.

"Hi, guys," said Alvin to the two boys. He grinned. "Pretty big day, huh?"

They grinned back. "We're out here to keep adults away until the party starts," said Shoie. "Mr. Wormley has turned the joint over to us, for as long as we want it." He opened the door for Alvin.

The cheer was so long and so loud that it shook a banana-split dish right off the shelf behind the soda fountain. Mr. Wormley, standing there in his white apron, looked down at it, then grinned and kicked the pieces to one side.

Theresa appeared from nowhere, and stood in front of Alvin with her hands raised to quiet the rest of the kids. Then, for Theresa Undermine, she did something very strange.

"Mayor Fernald," she said, "as Chairman of the Welcoming Committee I'm here to greet you. We, the kids of Miss Pinkney's class, are proud of our Mayor for a Day. And that's all the speech I'm going to make. So there. Now it's your turn."

For once in his life, Alvin was at a loss for words. Finally he started to laugh, and said, "Man! Wasn't that a sight, when Alicia and Peanuts let go of that tractor tire?"

Loud cheers and laughter. Peanuts Dunkle clasped his hands above his head like a prizefighter.

At that moment the door opened and in walked Miss Pinkney, with Dad right behind.

"Hi, kids," said Miss Pinkney, looking around the room. It was the first time that Alvin had ever heard her use the word. In class she always addressed them as "boys and girls, or "children."

"I figured I'd find you here celebrating," explained Dad. "And I also figured you'd like to have Miss Pinkney join you, as long as she sponsored your city government."

Someone shouted, "Speech! Speech!"

"No, I won't make any speech," she said. "But I would like to say how proud I am of all of you."

Worm, who was acting as host because it was his old man's ice-cream parlor, proudly took Miss Pinkney's arm and led her to one of the tables. The kids were silent until she was seated.

Mr. Wormley, standing behind the soda fountain, coughed to break the spell. "Okay, kids. Ice cream sundaes are on the house. It isn't every day that a man's son gets to be Police Chief!"

"Wait!" said Alvin. "Mr. Wormley, it's mighty nice of you to offer to treat all us kids. But we really want to pay for our own sundaes. You see, we set aside the money, from our own city treasury, to pay for them." Suddenly doubt struck him. He looked across the heads of the kids toward Alicia, his City

Treasurer. She smiled, and nodded her head just a bit. "So you total up the bill, Mr. Wormley, and let me know how much it is."

"Okay," said Mr. Wormley. "If that's the way you *really* want it. Now all of you line up here in front of me—you, too, Miss Pinkney and Sergeant Fernald—and tell me what you want."

After passing through the line, Alvin took his hot-fudge sundae to a table, where he and the Pest were joined by Miss Pinkney and Alicia.

Miss Pinkney looked across at him. "I suppose you know that you're pretty famous around town now, Alvin."

He blushed. "Well, I guess we were pretty lucky to catch those criminals." He put down his spoon. "Miss Pinkney, something has been bothering me. For just one day I've been a part of the city government, and yet I found that our officials are a bunch of crooks. And we elected them. Does that happen very often?"

"Oh, Alvin, you mustn't think that!" Miss Pinkney was genuinely concerned. "In the first place, you found only *one* of our city officials who was bad. In the second place, even that is highly unusual in a town this size. Most government officials, everywhere, are honest, dedicated men. They deserve respect, not criticism. No, there are very few criminals, such as Mayor Massey, in government."

"Okay, Miss Pinkney. Don't sweat it." Alvin knew immediately that his slang phrase wasn't a very polite one. "I mean, if you say so, I'll take your word for it."

Mr. Wormley appeared at his elbow. "Mayor Fernald, here's the bill, as you requested."

Alvin looked at the slip of paper, and suddenly was disturbed. The bill was for $10.30. He'd told Alicia to dig up only $9.36. As he looked around the room he discovered why there was a difference. Miss Pinkney, Dad and the Pest were just finishing their sundaes.

"Alicia," he whispered, "how much money do you have?"

"Mayor, I have ten dollars and twenty-six cents. I thought you might need some extra, so I got a little more than you asked for."

"Put it on the table," he said.

Alicia turned over her purse, and the coins came tumbling out. He needed four cents more, so he took a dime from his own pocket. He looked up at Mr. Wormley. "Keep the change," he said, "and thanks for letting us meet here tonight."

As Mr. Wormley disappeared behind the cash register, Alvin asked Alicia, "How'd you get the money?"

"Well," she said, "I began thinking about the city. Then, somehow, I began thinking about the firemen. It seemed to me that the firemen, when they're not training or putting out fires, probably must be playing cards or watching TV. Then I began to think about all the bottles of pop they

must drink while they're sitting around. And then I began thinking about *empty* bottles.

"So I went over to the firehouse, and sure enough, they had a whole storeroom full of nothing but empty bottles. So I asked if I could have the bottles to help the city treasury, and they said sure, and even paid me two dollars to haul them away. So I borrowed my little brother's wagon and hauled them down the street to Grocerland and sold them for eight dollars and thirty-six cents. So I got ten twenty-six altogether. And I wonder if our *real* city government couldn't make a lot of money that way—by selling empty pop bottles—so we wouldn't have to pay any city taxes."

She'd just finished her story when Theresa announced loudly, from another table, that it was getting late, and that she had to get home or her parents would "absolutely go mad from worry." The kids reluctantly started for the door.

"There's one more thing," Dad said quietly, but everyone in the room heard him and stopped. "Alvin, perhaps you remember that teletype message from the FBI. It said that the city of Smithville, Florida, offered a reward of one thousand dollars for the apprehension and conviction of Massey. We'll have to wait for court action, but I imagine the reward money will be paid. It rightly belongs to you." He looked straight at Alvin. "What are you going to do with it?"

A thousand dollars! Alvin had forgotten all about the reward. Boy, what he could do with that much money! He'd buy boxes and boxes of baking soda to mix with vinegar for his rocket experiments. He'd get that new boomerang he'd seen in the sports shop. He might even buy the pulleys he'd need to motorize his bike with the old lawnmower engine.

Alvin jolted awake from his dreams, and found himself looking straight into Speedy's eyes. Speedy had a strange, expectant look on his face, as though he was trying to send a message without putting it into words. Alvin had worked so closely with Speedy during the past few weeks that, on many occasions, he actually could tell what Speedy was thinking before Speedy opened his mouth. And now, suddenly, he got the message coming from those turtle-eyes.

"That reward money belongs to *all* the kids of the class," Alvin said. "And I suggest that we contribute it to the city of Riverton, to help buy those two vacant lots for playgrounds. I think, too, that we should tell the city we want one of those playgrounds named for Miss Pinkney."

There was a moment of silence, broken by Speedy's soft voice. "And I suggest that we make sure the city names the other playground for Mayor Alvin Fernald."

"G-g-g-g-great!" shouted Worm. And that started the cheering.

It *was* the greatest thing that could happen to a Mayor, thought Alvin. Both pleased and embarrassed, he glanced at his watch, as though checking whether it was time to head for home.

8:15 P.M. Three hours and forty-five minutes until his term in office would end.

He wondered whether he could do anything about that new bus route in the little time left. The Magnificent Brain stirred into action, thinking about the problem.

Suddenly an idea flashed through Alvin's mind. Pretty wild, but it just might work. . . .

Mayor Alvin Fernald headed for the door.